No part of this publication may be reproduced, stored in a retrieval system, or transmitted in any form or by any means, electronic, mechanical, photocopying, recording, scanning, or otherwise, without the prior written permission of the publisher, except in the case of brief quotations within critical reviews and otherwise as permitted by copyright law.

NOTE: This is a work of fiction. Names, characters, places, and incidents are a product of the author's imagination. Any resemblance to real life is purely coincidental. All characters in this story are 18 or older.

Copyright © 2020, Willow Winters Publishing. All rights reserved.

# Declan & Braelynn

*"If you don't heal what hurt you, you will bleed on people who didn't cut you."*

*Unknown*

From USA Today and Wall Street Journal best-selling romance author, W Winters, comes a provocative tale of an exclusive club designed for wealthy sinners. It's a story crafted for those of us who crave the villain.

Not everyone knows about The Club, which is by design. The main floor entertains the elite. There are dim lights, stolen touches and liquor flows freely to ensure guests get exactly what they want. There are high-profile clients, cuffs and collars, contracts and secrets in every corner.

But it's what lies beneath these floors, down the spiral staircase, that intrigues me the most.

There's a man who stays shrouded in the shadows of the darkest rooms. In this world of sinful tastes, he is the ruler, the devil, the boss. Declan Cross.

I knew him once when times were different, and the years have changed us.

He makes me an offer, one that speaks to the very soul of my desire. One I can't say no to and one that changes everything.

# Tease Me Once

# Prequel

## Declan

"I said, get on your knees." My repeated command is murmured in a voice as soft as the dim light in the room. The dark wooden bench beneath her lets out a creak as her trembling limbs move ever so slightly.

She's still shaking from the last of her orgasm, but it isn't enough. There is no amount of pleasure I could give her at this moment that would steal the thoughts from her pretty little head.

At least that's what she told me; that's what earned her this punishment.

"You pushed me, Braelynn. What did you think would happen?" The question comes with the leather paddle moving from my right hand to my left. As the light shines down on her, her bare skin is highlighted. With my hand splayed on her stomach, I move her myself, but she's weak.

The sleepless nights of worry and all the ways this is going to end have destroyed the woman I know.

The curious woman who wanted to play with fire no longer looks back at me with the desire she once had. She's broken and burned. And it's all my fault.

Her back rises and falls with each deep breath she takes, her belly pressed against the bench and her fingers gripping the wood beneath her. Is she purposely disobeying? Or is she so lost now that it doesn't matter what I say ... maybe she's given up.

I haven't prayed in what feels like an eternity, but if God ever listened, if he ever cared, I pray she isn't so destroyed that I mean nothing to her anymore.

"On your knees, my little pet." My words are spoken with a softness that draws her doe eyes to mine. Tears fall from the outer corners of her eyes. Trailing the paddle up the curve of her ass and then higher, her thick lashes lower as she shudders.

Fuck. My pulse races and I swallow thickly from the sight of her.

She doesn't cry from the pain. It's because she can't escape. She saw something she shouldn't have, and the terror has never been more evident than it is tonight.

She's slow to move, and just when I think she'll obey,

she'll give me control, she'll let it all go and forget about the harsh reality, submitting to the pleasure I can give her, her shoulders hunch over and she buries her face between her forearms on the bench.

The leather paddle clatters to the floor at the same time a sob hits her, ruling this woman in a way I should be. Her cries take over, and the apology she utters is strangled as she covers her face.

*Fuck. Not my Braelynn.*

*Fuck!*

With one arm slipping around her waist and the other cradling her reddened ass, I lift her to my bare chest, needing the skin-to-skin contact, heat to heat. My bare feet pad quietly on the floor as I kiss her hair and move us both to the antique canopy bed. The one she picked out. Like everything else in this room, it's for her. It's all for her.

The mattress protests as I lay her down gently, careful with my motions as her ass rests against the sheet. Even that gentle graze causes her to wince, but it's hardly noticeable. All I can see is a woman desperate to stop. For it all to end and for what happened to disappear.

That's not the way my world works. And I selfishly dragged her into this.

Reaching up, she wraps her arms around my neck, pulling herself closer to me even though I know damn well pressing against the bed like that is only exacerbating the pain she's feeling.

Again, I remind myself, it's not the physical pain that's done this. It's the threat of what's to come.

With her breasts squeezed against my chest, her small frame pulled together tightly as she attempts to nestle every bit of her she can against me, I do what I can to calm her.

Shushing her, kissing her hair, rubbing soothing circles on her back. I hold her as close as she needs. As she settles, her body relaxes slightly, but she never stops clinging to me.

"I will protect you." My promise to her is whispered at the shell of her ear and she stills. My little pet looks up at me and I've never felt so cold in my life. Helpless, alone. I've never felt like a failure and less of a man than I do when she doubts me like she does.

She doesn't believe I can protect her. I can barely breathe as the realization takes hold.

"They're your family," she whispers. Her gaze says it all: she thinks if they want her gone, I will choose them over her. *She's wrong.*

Chills travel up my spine and I rip my gaze away from hers, hating the sight of her uncertainty in me. The only thing that moves in this damn room is the fan, the blades turning over and over as everything else darkens and blurs. Never stopping. *None of it ever stops.*

With my body cold, my anger coiled and every emotion running on high, I grit my teeth and give her the harsh command, "Get on your knees now."

Shock lights in her deep brown eyes and she's quick to move, her dark disheveled locks spilling over her shoulder. Not a bit of her touches me as she assumes the position. Her knees are spread the width of her shoulders, with her back perfectly arched the way I crave, so I can fuck her deeply. The groan of the bed matches the one of desire that runs through my chest as I climb off and then grab her ankles, moving her to the edge of the mattress. She gives the smallest of yelps at the sudden movement. Her initial instinct to grab hold of the sheets soon gives way to her obedience. With my feet on the floor, and her ass at the perfect height, I let my fingers trail down her slit. She's not ready for me, so I'll take my time.

With my fingers toying with her clit, I give myself the time I need as well.

A gentle moan of pleasure leaves her as her head falls slightly. My left hand splays on her hip, holding her there as a gentle reminder.

This is the deal. *She's mine.* Mine to do whatever I want with.

The possessiveness that runs deep in my blood heats as I lean forward, gripping her ass and feeling her cunt tighten as I do. The mix of pain and pleasure finally give her what she needs to submit to me.

Dragging my fingers up her back, I grip her nape with my left hand as I spread her arousal with the opposite hand.

"That's better, my good sweet girl."

She rocks back gently and I'm quick to reprimand her, fisting her hair at the base of her neck and pulling slightly, which forces her back to arch. She's fucking gorgeous like this, at my mercy and weak for me. Waiting on me. *Trusting me.*

I love her like this.

No. My heart beats once, heavy and exacting. I love her. I won't let them take her from me.

As I line up the head of my cock at her entrance, I lower my lips to her neck, nipping once and loving the chills that run along her skin. At the sensitive spot there, knowing my warm breath will cause her to shudder, I whisper, "I would kill for you. I would kill *anyone* for you."

It's not just a promise. I will kill for her. I will do whatever I have to for her.

It's only a fraction of a moment that passes before what I've said hits her and the realization reflects in her body language. With that I thrust inside of her deeply, all the way to the hilt and I take her savagely, fueled by her tortured cries of pleasure, reminding her exactly who she belongs to.

# Chapter 1

## Declan

They say we're brutal for this very reason.

"If he doesn't make the payment …" my brother Carter states and his knuckles tap on the hardwood maple desk in a rhythmic way. The pace is even, as is Jase's head when he nods, agreeing with the unspoken consensus. "…let's make it very public," Carter concludes, stressing the word *very*.

"Very," Jase repeats with a glint of a smile. As if it's comical to murder someone in a manner that's worthy of making the six o'clock news.

There's a sinking feeling in my gut, paired with a heat that dances along the back of my neck but I nod as well. This is what happens when someone screws us over. They're made into an example, and lately the examples have been adding up.

Anytime there are shifts in power, we're bound to encounter challenges. They start off with small pushes against firm boundaries. We'd be naïve to think our enemies aren't constantly checking for cracks and tampering with well-defined barriers. If you let someone get away with one thing, they'll know they can get away with more.

"If he's even an hour late," Carter says, then gestures and Jase nods once again, this time adding, "Agreed."

My gaze moves from Jase's freshly shaven hard jawline to the bags under Carter's eyes. The recent arrival of Carter's firstborn, my nephew, has caused a stirring of betrayals.

My mother used to say, "Family will be the death of me." I don't remember much of her. She passed away when I was a kid, leaving the five of us behind, but I can hear her saying those words now. Her voice dripping with sarcasm as she rolled her eyes and tackled a never-ending cycle of dirty dishes and laundry.

There are only four of us now, and there's no doubt in my mind she would mourn for the men we've become.

Family may be the death of me, but they're all I have and I would give my life for them.

There's a bright flash against the paned window in the far corner of my office. Lightning strikes down, sending a streak of light through the expansive room. Even the darkened wood floors shine bright for a moment, revealing the polished and pristine surfaces. The room itself is free of clutter, and decorated with masculine tones of grays and browns. Black and white photographs Addison, Daniel's wife, took years ago are scattered around the room. Some of my late brother Tyler, and some of family before we became who we are today are in frames on the floor-to-ceiling shelves to my left. But the others are merely modern cityscapes of the places my sister-in-law has traveled. She helped me design the space.

Without her, lavish details like the gleaming bar cart and cut glass drawer pulls would not exist. Nor would the feminine touches designed for comfort, like the softness of the throw blanket on the corner chair, upholstered in buttery smooth amber leather.

"If Aaron doesn't pay, we'll make it obvious what our stance is moving forward."

"Execution style will do it," Jase states firmly, bringing the conversation back around. His dark eyes reach mine. Instinctively, I nod in return. They know whatever they choose, I will enforce with them. I'm the youngest, the most in debt in my mind. Not that they would ever hold anything against me. I'm more than aware I came out the lucky one, given what my oldest brothers endured after my mother died. The brutality of my father, then the barbarity of living through tragedy after tragedy.

"In the Romano alley on Fifth," Carter says and finalizes the location.

"He could still come up with the money," Jase suggests,

although he smirks at the thought, glancing down at his cuticles.

"With fifty thousand? Only if he steals it from someone else," I comment, knowing damn well it's within the realm of possibility and if it happens, someone else will kill the debtor. "Which I would greatly prefer."

There's a chorus of rough chuckles.

"That settles it then," Jase states although he shares a glance with Carter to be sure there's nothing else to discuss. It's nearly midnight and my evening is just getting started, although they'll go home and fall into bed with their wives who love them dearly.

With a deep exhale, Carter agrees. There's no more business to discuss.

"Give Aria a kiss for me, will you?" I tell Carter easily.

Jase's smile matches that of Carter's as he stands, slipping his hands into the pants pockets of his gray suit.

"It'd be better if you came home." Carter adds, "She misses you."

Jase piles on, "You should come home more often. We're starting to think you prefer it here."

I huff a humorless breath, although an asymmetric smile kicks up my lips. "It's quiet here and we all know there's work that needs to be done."

They go home to loving partners and children. I stay here, cleaning up the messes left behind. Monitoring the cameras that capture shit they shouldn't. Keeping tabs on the residents who peek outside their windows late at night and need to be reminded we're on their side.

The mafia only survives because of community. Crooks and murderers get away with their sins because of those who turn a blind eye, and those who support them.

Rubbing my eyes with the back of my hand, I say, "It's a fucking full-time job."

"You need help?" Jase offers and the sincerity rings clear in his tone.

"No. I need to figure out the last thing we discussed. Then I'll come home."

That sinking feeling in my stomach rears its ugly head again and both Jase and Carter's eyes darken, their lips setting into a thin line at the reminder.

There's a rat somewhere, leaking information to the feds.

"If you need anything," Carter murmurs and shrugs on his black jacket. It's bespoke and looks expensive as hell. Probably because it is. Both of my brothers dress in suits, stay cleanly shaven when in public. They represent the family well.

Daniel mostly sticks to the family estate, and I reside here most of the time. At The Club. My club. Everything I need is at my disposal.

Including concrete rooms in the basement, and alcohol upstairs for when I've finished tasks like taking care of late payments.

"Is there anyone or anything else I should be aware of?" I

question with Carter's back to me, his hand on the doorknob. He's quick to turn back around, Jase at his right. His dark eyes narrow as he thinks. My brothers look so alike. Tall, domineering. When they smile it's infectious, and when they're less than pleased, it's intimidating.

I see the way others react to them. I'm more like Daniel, quiet and preferring to keep to myself.

If anyone sees me, they wish they hadn't. That's how I prefer it.

Carter shakes his head and then peers at Jase before asking, "Am I forgetting anything?"

My chair protests with a groan as I shift my weight to focus on Jase, resting my ankle across my knee as I lean back.

"If anyone else comes in late on payments, we do the same."

"That was a given," I comment, knowing this weekend is going to be a bloody one. "It would match our reputation."

Carter says, "Our reputation is all we have."

"And each other," Jase adds. Carter nods, and again I note the darkness under his eyes from lack of sleep.

They say we don't wait, that we don't give second chances.

They say we're murderers and thieves. We're gangsters and lowlifes. Although, to be fair, we received those last two labels when we were only children. Poor and alone and not a sin worthy of hell yet to be made.

I think God would have forgiven us back then. We were barely aware of the world in those days. But now? We run this hell on earth.

"I'll tell Aria you're coming home this weekend." Carter's statement sounds like it's a question as he opens the door. Both of my brothers wait for my answering nod.

With that I bid them farewell, my gaze flicking to the whiskey in the corner of the room. To get through tonight, I'm going to need a stiff drink or two.

There's a common phrase people like to say: "Blood is thicker than water."

Its meaning has been twisted over time to convince others that family is most important. More important than anyone else. Because family is blood. The quote it's derived from entails the exact opposite: "The blood of the covenant is thicker than the water of the womb." The quote is meant to strengthen the bonds of soldiers on the battlefield. Those you spill blood with are closer to you than anyone else.

I've spilled more blood in the last decade than I ever thought possible alongside my brothers. There's not a damn thing in this world that could ever drive us apart. Blood and water, they are one and the same. We have killed for each other, we only survived because of it and the bloodshed will never stop.

It can't. If it does, it will be because we're buried under ten feet of dirt and only a stone will ever speak for us again.

Pouring three fingers of amber liquid into the tumbler, I throw it back. Tonight is just one of many similar evenings in the very near future. I can feel it in the very marrow of my bones.

# Chapter 2

## Braelynn

Life is brutal.

You can argue all you want that there are sweet parts of life. Some people cling to the belief that there are more good moments than bad, but that's not what I'm talking about. Life is brutal because it keeps on coming.

One hit after the other, knocking you down. You don't have time to get up and brush off the dirt.

Life doesn't acknowledge pain and the need to pause when it hits. We need to breathe, and life doesn't care. It doesn't stop and it doesn't grant reprieves.

In short: life can be a coldhearted bitch.

With a deep inhale, I follow a hairline crack in the ceiling of my new bedroom. My brow cocks at it, wondering if it's been there for years and it's fine, or if the crack will get worse.

The room itself doesn't feel like mine yet. There's not an ounce of me in it.

No vibrant colors, though the walls are primed a dull white. Brown boxes are stacked a few feet high and the only things I took out of them were the bedding. Which... leaves a lot to be desired.

The fitted sheet is pulled off the corner of my mattress, making an uncomfortable ridge under my foot. I push at it with my toes. I must have tossed and turned when I finally fell asleep last night.

That would explain why I don't feel rested at all. Par for the course, I suppose. Glancing at the clock, I realize the alarm hasn't even gone off yet. Nothing is worse than waking up feeling like shit before the sun has fully risen.

I debate on trying to slip back to sleep, but my mind is already reeling with every item on my to-do list. My bedroom is still barren, other than the mound of cardboard boxes. I have a hand-me-down bed frame and a nightstand my mom let me take. I have my mattress and a set of sheets that aren't too bad, fitted sheet notwithstanding. I have a laundry basket with my clothes in it, and not much else.

A numbness creeps over me and my tired eyes feel even more weighed down.

*Shake it off, Braelynn. Shake it off.* I remind myself that this isn't me. All of this doubt and exhaustion are because of what I've been through.

Today is different. Today is another chance.

I'm not going to be able to fall back asleep. And if I did, it wouldn't be dreams that greeted me. Sighing, I push the sheet halfway down my body and rub my eyes with the back of my hand. Once my brain is on for the day, it's on. There's no going back now. No matter how tired I am from last night.

It makes me hate my ex, Travis, all the more. It took forever to find sleep after he texted me. Just thinking his name makes my body go cold.

God, I don't want to think about that. Sure as hell not first thing in the morning.

The thoughts spun through my mind all night. I don't want to think about it; I'd rather focus on the crack in the ceiling, but I can't stop.

He gets drunk and messages me that he's sorry. It's a pattern. One that's destroyed the woman I used to be. My stomach sinks and my skin feels numb remembering all the times he's done it. He says he wants me back. If I answer anything at all, I only get more messages. More and more pressure.

I stopped responding months ago on the advice of my therapist, back when I left Travis for good and moved back in with my mother. It doesn't matter what he says. I'm not going to forgive him. I blocked him after many therapy sessions. It never feels good to block someone, to cut them out of your life with no intention of speaking to them again, but Tobias said it was healthy, that it was necessary. My therapist suggested going no contact, and setting the boundary lifted a weight from my shoulders. Until about ten hours ago.

Last night, Travis texted from a new number. I curl up onto my side under the blanket and squeeze my eyes shut harder. The sheer guilt and fear and anguish that cling to me are enough to make me wish I was dead.

*I know you moved out. I just want to talk …*

I know better than to think he just wants to talk. For the kind of man he is, talking is only the beginning. Give an inch and he'll take a mile, so I simply can't give him a damn thing.

The fact he's aware I moved sends a chill down my spine. Does he know I'm alone? That's the first question that came to mind. He knew enough to text me from a new number. Travis … he scares me. Even though I don't want to admit it.

I could change my number … again. But that means spending all afternoon conversing with some guy in a red polo shirt at the phone place and probably getting upsold on a plan I don't need. Even if I did, he might get the new number, and then what?

Travis doesn't stop. He doesn't let things be. I could say goodbye a hundred times and it would mean nothing. I swallow the lump in my throat and throw off the sheet entirely, feeling far too hot and far too suffocated.

I'm going to have to keep blocking him forever.

The thought of him keeping tabs on me scares me to death. It's what kept me up at night. He doesn't take no for an answer. It was hard enough when we broke up. It didn't seem like there was anywhere to go, and I ended up crashing with my mom until I could sign a lease.

The damn alarm sounds off just now. The wretched beeping is my savior. It keeps me from spiraling. Slamming my hand down, I remind myself of the same thing I've been saying for weeks now.

*I need to stay positive.*

That's what I need to do.

Breakup or not, living with my mom or not, small house or not—wallowing in those feelings won't get me where I need to go.

On the bright side, I have a new address. I've got enough money together for the deposit and the first month's rent and I'm here, I'm doing it. My life might look a little plain, but it's mine.

I drift on the bed for a few minutes, traveling through memories and emotions, a pillow between my legs as I stare aimlessly at the wall. As my toe meets the elastic band, I seethe. This fitted sheet is a real problem. When I get everything together again, I'm going to get a set of sheets that's the right size for the mattress so it doesn't come off in the middle of the frickin' night.

That's a good goal, and simple. I visualize moving down

the aisle at Target, looking at the pastel hues of the sheets, everything in a neat row. I know they're just sheets, but it's the little things. At twenty-five years old, I've never lived by myself. It was always dorms or roommates ... or Travis.

Life keeps coming and coming and coming and it hurts like hell, but at least a girl can get a new set of sheets.

Letting out a huff of a laugh, I open my eyes and hop out of the bed. My phone waits on my nightstand, plugged into its charger, and I pick it up without hesitation.

I have two text messages.

My heart pounds, thinking one of them might be from him. It might be a threat even. It wouldn't be the first time. I swipe the screen and open them up as fearlessly as I can, only to find they're from my friend Scarlet, and my mom.

The relief is palpable and I wish it wasn't.

Scarlet messaged at the ass crack of dawn. She's a good friend, but also a runner who doesn't understand that not everyone wakes up at 6:00 in the morning to exercise. She's also my hero because she got me my new job. Today I am a cocktail waitress. Which is far better than being a cashier at Travis's pharmacy. Worlds better, in fact, because he wouldn't dare set a foot in The Club.

*Scarlet: Reminder, don't be late and wear something sexy!! Higher tips that way, and you might meet someone ;)*

I send her back a kissing emoji and heart eyes, then open the message from my mom.

*Mom: Good luck today! Te amo, Braelynn <3*
*Braelynn: Te amo, Mama <3*

I reply immediately to my mom, even if her message brings down the corners of my lips. She begged me not to move out. She loves me, wants to be both my best friend and a mother hen, but I need out. I need to stand on my own two feet. My mom would keep me home forever if she could. Especially after what happened with Travis. My father would understand if he were still here. I need space. I need independence. I love her dearly, but I need to be okay on my own.

Even if I'm not exactly truthful about the place I'll be working. I said waitress ... I just didn't mention it was at The Club. There are rumors and gossip about that place. But they were hiring and Scarlet said she could get me in. She said they pay well and Lord knows I need to get back on my feet. My phone vibrates and I look at the screen to see my mom's messaged me again with a thumbs-up emoji.

I love that she's thinking of me. I can practically feel the luck suffusing the air around me, almost like I was still living with her. My mama is my hero. Always and forever.

Padding into my bathroom to shower, I run through the pep talk I've been practicing.

New life.

New apartment.

New job.

With both hands on the edge of the sink, I stare at my

reflection. "Today is the first day of the rest of my life."

It's painful to start over, but discomfort is part of growth. I can handle anything that comes my way today. I will handle anything that comes my way today. Everything that came before makes me strong enough to do this.

My hands tighten on the edge of the granite counter.

And this time, it's all mine. This is my shampoo and my shower and my hot water. All of which I paid for. Nobody else is choosing it for me or holding power over me with it. That sick, pricking chill plays at the back of my neck remembering how Travis did just that.

Biting down on my lower lip, I feel shame. It took me far too long to realize that to him, it was his money, so he could treat me however he wanted.

That was then. This is now.

This new job, a high-end cocktail waitress, as Scarlet called it, could turn out to be great. If I can figure out how to work the system like Scarlet says, I'll have more money in my pocket and even more freedom.

I'll get that new set of sheets. They won't come off the corner of my mattress. Maybe I'll even get a cute lamp to boot. I smile into the water as I scrub down my face, thinking about it. Smooth sheets and no tossing and turning at night. That's what I'm aiming for. Peace and freedom. You know what? I can get those things. There's nothing stopping me now.

The bathroom is about as barren as my bedroom, but I've

got what I need to do my hair. A blow-dryer and a curler and hairspray and hours of practice. I spend more time than usual in front of the mirror. I won't let Scarlet down and be late, but I'm showing up as the new version of me.

With plenty of concealer under my eyes.

When my hair's perfect, I practice my polite smile into the mirror.

*They'll fall in love with you*, Scarlet promised. It's a pity how much that made me feel cherished. Just the thought of strangers loving me was enough to sway me into taking the job.

I stop my thoughts in their tracks, clicking off the curling iron. *Positive thoughts only.* I'm not going to think of my ex or the hard climb ahead of me, or the possibility I might fail out of this new job.

Nope. I'm going to succeed. I can't keep running back to my mom's house every time life gets hard. I need to build my own safety net, and it starts with this new job. It's natural to be nervous about it. The stakes are high. Life keeps coming no matter what I do, so I just need to keep going. Day in and day out. All I have to do is survive.

I bypass the basket of laundry and stride to my closet. There's one dress hanging inside, one that Scarlet helped me pick out. Staring at the pile of boxes, I roll my eyes. I know, I know. I need to unpack. At the top of my to-do list is the need to put away my clothes and make this place into a real home, instead of a temporary stopping place. This is my home. This is my new home, and my new life, and I'm going to be fine.

With the satin slipping through my fingers, I take in the deep red. The dress is a dark, dark red. Shivers run up and down my arms at the feeling of the fabric. This dress is my uniform for the evening.

It makes me feel like a different woman. I turn in front of the mirror, letting the cloth drape down my body. It makes my dark hair stand out, and I get a thrill of pride that I managed to make myself look like this. Sexy and mysterious and in control.

They'll never know how scared I am, deep down. No one will ever know. Because I'll put on a smile that goes with this dress. That reminds me of the lipstick. Scarlet inspired me to get it. She told me red is a confident color. Perched atop the worn wood of my dresser is a little striped bag from Sephora. A spray of tissue paper pokes out of the top and nestled inside is my new lipstick.

I take it back to the bathroom mirror and apply it.

The shade of the lipstick matches the dress perfectly. That's the last piece of my uniform and I did it exactly right. It's hard to match colors so exact, so the forty-five minutes I spent in the store going back and forth between different shades is paying off. I stare at my own face in the mirror until I look like a stranger. A beautiful stranger who could be anyone she wants to be.

My phone vibrates on the bedside table out in the bedroom, and I go back out to see who messaged me.

**Scarlet: How is everything going? Just checking in ...**

**Braelynn: *I'm all ready. Heading out soon!***

I can't help the feelings that come over me. It's comforting to have someone who's concerned about me like Scarlet is. Gratitude is overwhelming. We've known each other for years, but only recently got as close as we are. Since everything started breaking down with Travis, she's really been there for me when I needed it.

**Braelynn: *See you soon.***

One last stop at the mirror. I've made myself as perfect as I could for this. Perfect red dress. Perfect lipstick. It's the lipstick, most of all, that gives me courage. I'll fake it 'til I make it. I'll fake it until every dark thing that's ever happened to me is far away in the rearview mirror. I'll fake it until there's more happiness than pain in my life.

Blinking away every insecurity, I focus on the comic relief: I'll fake it until I get that new set of sheets.

With a roll of my eyes and a huff of a laugh, I focus on that one small goal to send me on my way. It'll feel good to have those new sheets, and better to sleep through the night without worrying.

The woman in the mirror is who I'll be when that happens. No more Braelynn who cried all the way home to her mother's house. No more Braelynn who doesn't want to face the day and lets her lover treat her like a doormat.

No more Braelynn who's so afraid she can't even sleep at night.

# Chapter 3

## Declan

The office door shuts with a quiet thud and I lock it as I always do. The keys clink as I test the lock.

It's only as I turn that I realize I've forgotten my tie on my desk. Pausing, I gaze down at my attire: gray slacks, a black leather belt that matches the onyx of my oxfords and a burgundy button-down. The din from up the iron spiral staircase tells me The Club is already bustling with clients.

*Fuck it.*

I drop the keys into my pocket and then run my hand along my jaw. Stubble lines my chin, but that's how I prefer it. I'm not interested in the typical dick-measuring contests men tend to have at nightclubs. Every other man who walks through those doors can feel superior behind the closed doors of this establishment. The liquor flows for them in the private dining areas. Women dance in burlesque shows and provide ... other entertainment.

Most importantly, they're comfortable conducting business here. Upstairs is for deals. Handshakes are exchanged, money is passed under tables. All arrangements are dealt with discretion.

And we remain aware of every business transaction and affair that matters in this city and the four corners beyond it. Ever since Marcus left, we've taken the role of providing communication efforts for men in our profession. With the clank of my shoes smacking against the iron, I peek down the hall from my office.

If everyone knows upstairs is where major deals on the East Coast are done, they know downstairs is where people go for not holding up their agreements. The private rooms are mostly furnished for all manner of sin. If ever the police raided, which they have before, there are plenty of women who escort the men in here to testify that they enjoy their partners in the privacy of those rooms. In fact, there are only two that are concrete from wall to wall with a drain in the center of the room.

As I push the door to the main floor open, I smirk, remembering the latest officer's brow cocking as I described what "water sports" were and that our club doesn't judge kinks so long as men clean up after themselves. Every so often the cops make a pathetic attempt at shutting us down. As far as the authorities are concerned, I run a gentleman's club with playrooms in the basement. Everything is consensual and the books are clean. The numbers are balanced when it comes to what we show.

It's easy to pass money through, moving around whatever amounts are needed for certain deals. The devil is in the details, as they say.

The majority of our guests are on the up-and-up. There may be whispers of what occurs, but they're all rumors. The most perverse allegations that have been proven are politicians who've brought their mistresses to The Club. There is no exception to what manner of debauchery we allow, so long as phones are left at the door with their coats and every check is paid.

The Club is my creation, my contribution to my family and the only way I've been able to stay on top of things while my brothers have stepped back.

They've moved on in life in a number of ways. They have children and lives I've never imagined for myself, let alone for them. I've taken on more of their burdens and more of what comes with this line of business.

Even Seth, my best friend, is no longer available like he used to be. His son is almost two now. My godson.

I do every damn thing I can for all my family, including maintaining our ruthless reputation.

The music is alluring, a downtempo mix that offers the same ambiance as the dim lighting and lit candles on every table. The white wax provides a stark contrast against the black linens.

From this entrance, the stage, which is empty at the moment, is to my right. In front of me are the folding seats, separated into isolated sections, with the bar behind it. The hall leading to the entrance is to my right. It's private and discreet, although the tables are full of unsuspecting patrons at the moment.

"Good afternoon, Mr. Cross," Scarlet greets me, tipping her chin down as she passes by. Her lips pick up into a simper, but her eyes don't reach mine. As she slips past, balancing the silver tray in her left hand with empty wineglasses and stacked plates, I peer across the room.

There are a dozen tables filled, another dozen empty. A few tables consist of men in sharp suits toasting, while a few have groups of women, dripping of wealth in designer dresses and handbags. Most tables are occupied by couples, though, preparing for a night out and having chosen this destination, more than likely, for the rumors of what's happened behind these closed doors.

Scarlet and Angela are working the floor, both in short, deep red dresses. We allow black, white, or a specific shade of red. It's an unwritten rule, one not explicitly stated anywhere. But the colors have distinct meanings.

White is worn if a staff member is interested in playing, but has limits. Hard limits. It's often soft touches, or heavy petting at the most. It's a tease, nothing more.

Black indicates the waitress, server or anyone wearing the color is off-limits. No touching whatsoever.

Mia, the bartender currently occupied with cleaning the necks of the liquor bottles, has always worn black. She's slim and tall, with a deep V-neck dress that displays her cleavage generously. Her jet-black hair is twisted into a tight bun at the nape of her neck. She never wears an ounce of color, not even in her makeup.

Once a patron assumed the uniform color had no meaning. He quickly found out he was wrong and that when she said no, it meant no.

The security who stood at the curtained entrance was useful that night in coloring that gentleman's eyes black also.

Glancing toward my left, I note Jeffrey and Nicholas are working tonight as well. They're nothing but muscle, disguised in black suits and polite nods.

"Good morning, sir," Angela greets me as I get to the bar, a smile playing on her lips.

My eyes drift down her dress, a tsk at my lips. "It's well after noon, Angela," I say, correcting her with a playful tone.

The red dress has a deep V that ends at the woman's navel. Which is the third color we allow and the most preferred. Red informs the patrons the woman is available for whatever the men would like.

I don't play where I work, but I have to admit I've been tempted more than once, in my weaker moments. Angela is very aware I'm not interested. Just as I'm aware she is a flirt with everyone and prefers Mia to any of the men she toys with.

Whatever arrangement they have is none of my business.

"Good afternoon then," Angela replies and I don't miss Mia's gaze following her ass as Angela leaves.

"Coffee, Mr. Cross?" Mia questions.

"Please." She's worked for me since the doors opened two years ago, as have a good number of the staff.

Everyone is replaceable, though, and multiple bodies have come and gone since then. One constant is the women. There are a number of rumors surrounding the club and the one I love the most is that the women run this place. That they have the men wrapped around their little fingers. They make the rules, and they're protected by myself and my brothers.

We've proven that more than once. Of all the whispers, I prefer those the most.

Which leads my gaze to land on curves that sway with a deep red dress clinging to every inch of a new waitress. And then she turns.

"Would you like your usual as well?" she questions a patron, but I hardly hear her. The music fades to nothing as her long dark brunette hair falls down her tanned shoulders, teasing along the slender curve of her neck. Time slows as the memories come back to me.

Braelynn.

"Who's that?" I say even though I'm certain it's her. Her plump lips match the deep red shade of the satin dress. I knew her years ago, in a different life, although it seems both of us have grown since then. My pulse quickens as I take in every inch of her. The world around me stands still for a moment as the scene comes back to me when I first met her. Her father's as Irish as they come. Her mother, Latina. Braelynn's temper comes from them both, her beauty, though ... her dark eyes and curled messy hair are uniquely hers. Although both seem tamed as my gaze begs for her to look back at me.

As my blood rushes in my ears, I hear her laugh at something the woman she's waiting on says. It's feminine and quiet but it's her. Every bit of her that I remember.

*Braelynn.*

"Scarlet's friend," Mia says just as Angela makes her way to us once again, a drink order slip in hand.

"The new girl?" she says and follows my gaze to her.

"What's her name?" I ask, my tone low and my question holding a demand that catches both women off guard.

"Braelynn," Mia answers. Angela's eyes hold a curiosity I don't care for.

It takes a calm control to keep the statement on the tip of my tongue. I know her.

When my mother died, she was the only one to tell me she was sorry. It was barely a murmur, her hand grazing mine. And then she was gone and my life changed forever.

"Braelynn." I speak her name out loud and nearly choke on it. All the while, she doesn't even notice me.

The ceramic saucer and mug clink as Mia cautiously sets down my coffee on the white marble bar top.

"Tell her to come to my office," I instruct Angela, who stares back at me with wide eyes. She doesn't hold back her surprise. A stray blond curl falls in front of her face and she brushes it away as disappointment registers in her gaze.

"Do you have something to say?" I keep my question spoken slowly, my gaze piercing through hers. Her eyes widen ever so slightly as Mia takes a hesitant step back.

Color drains from Angela's face as she shakes her head, gently swaying her halo of curls.

"'Cause it looks like you have something you want to say," I add in a deadly low tone. My personal life is none of her concern.

She speaks in a single breath, her chest barely rising and falling. "Not at all, Mr. Cross."

"Good. Send her to my office when she has a moment." Giving the command, I gather the mug and leave. Not sparing either of them, or Braelynn, a single glance.

# Chapter 4

## Braelynn

This lipstick is doing me all kinds of favors. It was worth the twenty bucks after all.

Men's eyes slip down to look at it and women compliment me on it, and altogether it feels like I am doing all right for my first shift at The Club.

Even though this place is nothing like I imagined. Scarlet said it was like a high-end speakeasy. Like being taken back in time, but it isn't.

It's modern. It's expensive. It's like the devil designed this place. There's a small kitchen, but the food they serve looks like it belongs in one of those fancy restaurants you see in magazines and TV shows.

All of this is so far out of my league.

My shoulders stay pulled back when Scarlet reminds me to carry myself like I belong here. And I do. It feels like I'm supposed to be here. Which doesn't make a damn lick of sense, because a place like this is merely a dream to someone like me.

"Keep it up," Scarlet says and winks at me as we pass each other. She's got a martini glass in her hand and I've got a bill in my left.

It takes me a moment to remember the passcode and how to navigate the system. I'm slow, but it's my first day and the bartender, Mia, she's there to help.

It's a bit too good to be true, but all of them point out that it gets more intense at night. Things are expected to be busier and louder, with everything moving faster. So I have about four hours to get familiar. Glancing down at my heels, I grimace. My toes curl in the tips of them. The first chance I get, I'm slipping into flats. Tips be damned.

I didn't realize the extent of how short my dress was until I leaned down to take someone's order and a breeze slipped between my thighs. It may have made me blush and yank the fabric down the moment I got away, but the tips, even for just five tables, have been insanely good. Scarlet wasn't kidding about that. I'll have that new set of sheets and new bedroom furniture in no time.

Slips are returned, orders paid, new guests are seated and greeted. Everything is fairly comfortable and easygoing.

The other women are kind. The men in sharp suits who stand at the front ... they're intimidating until they look at me. It's all polite smiles, but there's no doubt in my mind they can be brutal.

I don't know all their names yet, but I know the bartender is Mia; there's a man in the kitchen named Benji and the other waitress working right now is Angela. The best way to describe her is that she's an assassin with long, curly blond hair. She moves faster than Scarlet and me combined and she's already nudged me to let me know if I fall behind she can help. Her experience is obvious and a number of the men seem to know her by name.

Maybe in that way it's like a speakeasy. There are quiet conversations but most of the people here know everyone by first name.

Maybe ... I shake my head, unsure of myself. It's an odd mix and it's hard to put my thumb on what exactly is throwing me off.

By two hours in, I'm starting to feel a little surer of myself. At four hours in, it's slowed down a bit. Mia assures me as I walk off with a round of shots for two men in the corner, that it's the eye of the storm.

"Get ready, the intensity is about to pick up."

One deep breath in, and I tell myself I can do this. I am doing this.

Slipping out my lipstick, I touch up the color and then I

spot Scarlet off to the side talking to Angela. Their heads are together and when they see me coming, Scarlet nods to her and approaches me.

"Hey," I start, "I think things are—"

"Mr. Cross wants to see you in his office," she says as soon as she's close enough. Scarlet holds a black tray close, flat against her body.

The air leaves my lungs. Cross. There's a faint numbness that goes to my fingers. I knew the Cross boys. I knew of them. And Scarlet told me they own this place. Everyone knows of them, or at least the word on the street is that they run this entire town.

"Mr. Cross?" I question and if I had more strength, I'd ask which one. My heart races and my blood chills.

"Yes." Scarlet nods once, her gaze staring at mine as if I'm being slow. "He wants to see you in his office."

*Which one?* The question begs to be asked, but it stays at the back of my throat, choking me. Standing there expectantly, she doesn't seem nervous in the least.

"Is everything okay?" I question and she lets out a laugh.

"I'm sure it's fine," she answers and that's not reassuring even a tiny bit. My pulse picks up, nervousness pricking along my skin.

*Which Cross brother is it?*

That's not the question that comes out. "Where is his office?"

She gestures at a nearby matte black door. It's disguised

into the wall, the knob of it cut glass. It's expensive, just like everything else in this place.

And it leads to *him*. I stop myself right there, breathing in deeply. It leads to a Cross brother. It doesn't mean him. He probably won't even recognize me. He didn't know me then. He sure as well wouldn't know me now.

"Through there and down the spiral staircase. There are some rooms down there for … certain things." Scarlet shrugs, blushing. It throws me off-balance to see her face go red like that and I'm thankful for the distraction.

She knows this place, so whatever goes on down there must be shocking even by her standards.

"Certain things?" The question falls from my lips eagerly in my rush to think of anything other than a boy I once knew. Still, I'm taken aback at the color in Scarlet's face. She's hiding something from me. "What certain things?"

Scarlet glances around us, checking to see if anyone is listening. She leans in close to me and drops her voice. "Look, some of these guys … they're hot. And they're willing to pay for other things, you know?"

Heat rushes to my face. Oh my God. I must be as red as she is. My imagination spins through all the possible scenarios of the rooms downstairs. "Certain things" sounds illicit and maybe illegal. The question comes out in a hushed whisper as I grab her arm, pulling her in closer. "You sleep with them?"

"Not all of them. Some of them I like to ... enjoy, and I do." Scarlet glances around the club, taking in the women laughing over their wine and the reclined men in expensive suits. Her gaze lands on a couple across the room. They can't take their eyes off each other. "Sometimes couples come, and we ... take them down there to enjoy themselves. Sometimes they want company, sometimes not. There's also the entertainers." Scarlet straightens her back. "This is a judgment-free zone. If you want to do something here, you do it."

My immediate response comes out in a single breath. "Well, I don't want to." Is that what they expect of me? "This isn't what—"

Her hand lands on mine as she reassures me, "Relax, it's not ... it's not required. It's just something that happens sometimes."

"I don't want to—"

Again she cuts me off. "You say that now," Scarlet murmurs, a smile playing at the corners of her lips, "but when it's late, the liquor is flowing, and these men look at you like they've never wanted anything more ... sometimes it's tempting." She shrugs and adds, "If we want something, and they want it too ..." her words drift off as her gaze lands on a man in a gray suit, seated by himself. Her tongue sweeps across her lower lip and she says, "All I'm saying is," it's then her eyes meet mine again, "don't knock it 'til you try it."

"I'm not judging, but if I still don't want to?" I question

although I can't get the rest of it out. My mind is spinning and I can barely focus on anything. I need to know whether she's telling the truth. If it's a requirement that I sleep with men ... or couples ... in those rooms downstairs, then I have to find another job.

I can serve drinks and take orders, I can flirt even and have a good time in that regard, but I draw the line there. Even if Scarlet thinks I might like more.

Scarlet puts her hand on my arm in a comforting gesture. "If you still don't want to, you don't have to. But you do need to go to the boss's office."

Fuck. Heat rises to my cheeks hotter than before. I swallow hard. "So why does he want me to go down there?" I nearly choke on the question and again, a little voice whispers in the back of my head. *Which Cross brother?*

"That's just where his office is. You'll see. It's straight ahead once you get down the stairs. His door is the red one." Her eyes dart to my lips then back up to meet my gaze. "It matches your lipstick."

"Does he expect me to sleep with him?" If his office is downstairs, with all those other rooms, then ...

"No." Scarlet shakes her head. "No. Mr. Cross doesn't ... he keeps his dick off the table." Her arms cross over her chest as she makes the statement, giving her cleavage an added boost.

"What does he want?"

"I don't know." Her answer comes out with less patience

than before. Scarlet takes a few steps to the bar and stacks her tray there. She's always taking inventory of the club, making sure no one needs anything. "He doesn't usually ask for anyone, but maybe it's just 'cause you're new. I'll watch your tables while you're down there."

With her easy tone, I give her a short nod and take in an uneasy breath. Faux courage all the way.

"Okay."

Time slows down as I open the door, and when I close it, the world that feels like something else is muted and I'm met with only descending stairs and silence. Taking the steps one at a time, I go down the staircase. It's heavy iron in a spiral shape and my heels seem to wobble with every step. At the bottom is a hallway. Expensive paneling lines the walls. It's not like a basement. It's less like a fancy speakeasy that the upstairs resembles and far more like private property. It feels like someplace you'd need a password to get into. A passing thought is haunting. If the devil owned real estate on the East Coast, and a sinner perished, I imagine this could very well be the modern gates of hell. Sconces line the walls, the pattern mimicking the spiral staircase. Every small detail drips of wealth.

I swallow thickly and head toward the dark red door near the end of the hall. My heels click in the quiet hall in a menacing way. The echo mocks my racing heart.

Again I wonder which brother I'll see. Vaguely, I imagine

it'll be nothing like the dreams I've had occasionally for years.

The door is in front of me before I know it and I hesitate, my nerves churning in my gut. I knock as confidently as I can.

"Come in." His voice is deep, his command firm and my body obeys.

The glass knob is cold as I open the door. The door swings easily, not protesting what feels like a sinful act. My dress has ridden up from walking down the stairs and I tug at the hem as I walk in, thankfully hidden by the door. I take a quick glance down to make sure my hem is in place, then look up to see the man at the desk.

My heart skitters, forgetting its beat when his eyes find mine.

I know him. A chill runs down my skin and time pauses, only for a moment.

It's the youngest brother, Declan. I'd recognize his eyes anywhere. The curve of his jaw is sharper and lined with a five-o'clock shadow.

He's no longer an impoverished boy with dark clouds in his eyes.

The man looks more expensive than the office, and this office ... Dark wood gleams underneath framed prints of cityscapes, and all the neutral colors work together to highlight the man at his desk. He stands up from his seat, revealing a tall, muscular body in a tailored button-down. He strides slowly around to the front of his desk and leans against it. Heat crawls down the back of my neck. I knew him before, but this isn't the person I knew. This man is radiating power and control.

He looks me up and down. "It's quite a short dress."

"Declan—"

"Most go with Mr. Cross."

"I'm sorry." My lips feel oversensitive, almost numb. I can barely move, let alone control the words tumbling from me. Intimidation does not at all do this moment justice.

"Don't be." His eyes roam over me, undressing me. "If that's what you want to call me."

I flush violently. I'm as red as my dress now. Gathering my composure, I remind myself that I'm working. This is a job. A loud tick reminds me that time continues on. It moves and so should I. "You wanted a drink?"

"No."

My fingers lace between each other in front of me as I stand just in front of the doorway, the light from the hall still filtering in. *Please don't ask me to close it.* That's all I can think. I don't know what I'd do with myself if I were locked in with him.

I question with my tone relatively even, "Is there something I can do for you, then?"

"I'm sure there is." His fingers toy with something on his desk. A small metal die, I think. He hasn't taken his eyes off me since I stepped into the room. Everywhere his gaze lands, it burns my skin. "You just started today?"

I nod, clearing my throat.

"You have questions."

"I just started so there are some, but I'm learning quickly." It's so quiet between us, I'm certain he can hear me swallow.

"Scarlet referred you?"

"Yes."

He nods. "Did she suggest you wear red or did you decide that on your own?"

I'm overheating in his presence. It would be rude to look away from him, but he's so striking that I want to close my eyes. Simply glancing in his direction gives him some kind of power over me.

Even worse, my mind keeps trying to compare him to the boy he was, but it's impossible in the face of the man he's become. His question hangs in the air between us. It wasn't as casual as he made it sound. I know that much, at least.

"Scarlet said I could wear red or black or white." I don't want to say anything to get Scarlet in trouble. She told me the colors to choose from, and I chose. Although she told me I looked best in red.

"Scarlet told you that?"

"Yes." She also told me shorter was better, but maybe I didn't go short enough. Scarlet and Angela are both wearing shorter dresses than I am. Or maybe, as the new girl, I'm supposed to wear something longer. "Is my dress okay?"

Declan stares me in the eye. "Red means you'd like to be fucked."

Shock blanks out my mind in a cold realization, followed by embarrassment. There's a rushing sound in my ears that won't go away. People have seen me, up there in the club. I've been waiting tables. Every man who smiled at me thought I was offering to come downstairs with him. "Excuse me?"

Declan smirks at me, setting the die down. "I imagine Scarlet didn't tell you that."

"She didn't." My nerves react with anxiousness. "And that is not why I wore this—" I swallow a burst of fear. "I'm not—" before I can explain myself, he cuts me off.

"From now on, I'd like you to wear black. Don't ever wear red again." Declan narrows his eyes. "But you can keep the lipstick. If anyone asks for you tonight, inform them that the boss has requested you. Is that understood?"

It's quiet as I stare at him, taking in every word he's said as if it's a drug. It's an order. He's so commanding with his tone that it makes my knees go weak. Scarlet didn't tell me everything there was to know about The Club. She might be wrong about what Declan wants too. If he's requesting me now ...

"Say 'yes, sir,'" he prompts.

"Yes, sir."

His brow furrows like I've upset him somehow. It's not an expression I recognize from when I used to know him. He used to be soft and gentle. A good kid. Now there's a hardness to every detail of his expression. Life hasn't been kind to him. It's made him tougher. His eyes darken as he watches me in my red dress that he disapproves of. "No one touches you," he says.

"I—"

I'm interrupted from questioning him when his phone rings. Declan takes one look at the screen and puts it to his ear. "Yes," he says, his eyes still on me. I let out a breath. This is my cue to leave, my skin still prickling with a cautious unease. I shouldn't listen in on his calls. He's still on the phone as I turn to leave and grant him privacy.

"Braelynn." My name in his voice stops me with a shiver, the door halfway open with my hand gripping the frame. I turn back. Declan leans on his desk, in control and at ease with the situation. "It's good to see you."

My heart does that flip again. This time it hurts a bit more.

"It's good to see you too, Declan."

Rushing the words out, I move as quickly as I can. I shut the door behind me a second before my knees give out. My body sags against the deep red door, heart hammering. I can't catch my breath.

*Declan Cross.*

Being in the same room with him was nothing like I expected. *He remembered me.*

I didn't know he would look like that. His eyes feel like they're burning through the door even now, but I can't bring myself to stand upright.

Each command he gave repeats in my mind as I attempt to steady myself.

*I'd like you to wear black. Don't ever wear red again.*

*Inform them that the boss has requested you.*

It's a long moment before I can stand tall and straighten my dress once again. Every step takes me farther from his office, but I can feel him down there, as if something is calling for me, pulling me, tempting me and luring me back down to a place I can't imagine ever being again.

# Chapter 5

## Declan

Dark brown eyes and deep red lips flicker through my mind all night.

My fingers itch to grip her bare skin, lift her skirt up and toy with her. My cock aches, hard and desperate for relief at the thought of leaving marks on her ass. Spanking, whipping, fucking her deep and brutal.

A low groan leaves me, hating that I can't stop watching the cameras. Not for business, just for her. Every man who glances down the top of her red satin dress might as well be begging for me to cut their fucking throats.

She will never wear that color again.

My door opens without a knock. I don't have to look up to know it's Jase. Taking in a steadying breath, I rip my gaze away from Braelynn's curves and will my erection to knock it the fuck off.

Luckily, my brother's statement is helpful in that department. "We've been given the list of potential leaks and it includes your girl."

"My girl?" The back of my neck heats at what he's said, and if my expression gives away the fear, he doesn't seem to notice.

"Scarlet Miller," Jase states while taking a seat in the high-back chair across from my desk. He leans forward, his fingers steepled and his elbows resting on the desk. "There's a good chance she's the leak."

Heat dances along my skin. She referred Braelynn; she's close to her. My pulse quickens.

My objection leaves me without hesitation. "She's been here over a year."

Jase nods, opting to lean back in the chair, his thumb tapping on the armrest. "You know how they operate. It takes time before they slip."

I nod, meeting my brother's gaze but not liking it.

"Do you think it's just one?" I question, my gaze begging me to look back at the cameras, back at Braelynn as if simply seeing her will give me a yes or no to the question burning in the back of my mind.

Is she an undercover agent? Is she here to set me up?

Both God and the devil know she's a weakness for me.

Jase shrugs a heavy shoulder. "That's what we need you to focus on."

"Consider it done," I tell him.

"Do we already have surveillance?" he asks.

"Not outside of The Club. I'll set it up." Focusing on Miss Miller alone keeps my head clear. We'll install surveillance and trackers on her car, her phone and her residence. Everything. "It won't take long."

"We have to know what she has on us," Jase speaks and I nod, going over every step from the previous times we've dealt with someone who's snitched. It never ends well for them.

"Scarlet, though?" I question him again, narrowing my eyes as I tilt my head.

"That's what it seems like. If not her, it's someone else here. The books were mentioned."

A tension runs through my body. We can get away with murder easily enough, but money laundering is far more difficult.

Clearing my throat, I tell him, "I see."

"If history is anything to go by, they'll look into the numbers."

My mind slips back to Braelynn as I tell my brother, "We'll find a way to flush them out."

My brother drones on, his voice turning to white noise as I watch the cameras and in them see Scarlet with her hand on Braelynn's back.

There's a sinking feeling in my chest, one that weighs my breath down, making it harder to focus, harder to think of anything other than the possibility that she's come here to ruin me.

With my thumb resting on my bottom lip, I will her to answer me the question. *Did you come here to destroy me, Braelynn?*

I remember her well, the girl I used to know. But we all change, don't we?

"I'll get to the bottom of it," I tell Jase, dragging my gaze away from her. "Whoever it is, they won't be a problem for long."

The hours drift by slowly. Jase forwarded the report he paid an officer for when he got word there was someone on the inside. It pays to have the higher-ups in your back pocket.

All we need to do is stay one step ahead of them. They may have someone watching us, but we have dozens watching them.

The black and white text on the computer screen has stared back at me, taunting me and every move I've made since opening the doors to The Club. According to the report, they need evidence before getting approval for a bust. The feds have an estimated timeline of six months. Which means Scarlet, and any other witnesses, need to be long gone by then so their testimony is irrelevant and, in that time, we can't slip up.

There's not a doubt in my mind it's a waitress here who's given the information in this report. There are details about deals that have gone down exclusively in the dining room upstairs. No one makes a move without our approval and the money that's been exchanged is well documented.

Running my hand through my hair, I lean back and take a deep breath.

It's all hearsay at this point, no proof. If there's no hard evidence, they have to rely on witnesses. Which begs the question, which one of them is it?

A whisper tickles the back of my mind. *Is Braelynn involved?* I don't believe in coincidences and the timing isn't on her side. Scarlet was around for every one of the documented testimonies in this report. And Braelynn is guilty by association.

That doesn't explain why I flick back over to the monitor, watching her tempting curves as she leans over the bar counter, reaching for a cocktail napkin.

A deep groan resonates in the back of my throat.

It's late. The singer this evening is already gone, leaving a lone mic on the stage.

Three a.m. is only minutes away, and most of the waitresses have left with their chosen date for the evening. Scarlet's laid over the lap of a man she's been with more than once.

I don't ask details. I don't involve myself in what the women do. What my employees choose to do after hours is their business, not mine.

Although it doesn't hurt my bottom line.

Clicking through the cameras, I account for each and every one of the patrons and employees.

All is well, with one exception. There is a table of three men, one of them eyeing Braelynn. Heat pricks up the back of my neck. She's already told them the boss requested her.

They've already paid their bill.

Smiles and laughter may accompany their table, but the two drunkest can't seem to drag the third away. The one requesting the napkin from Braelynn.

I could sit here and watch on the cameras. I can already see it playing out in a number of ways.

She denies the man again, and they leave, easy enough.

She denies them and they don't leave, in which case, my security escorts them out. They're already watching just as I am.

Those are the only two possibilities. Yet I find myself rising from my chair, my jaw clenched as I push open my door, not bothering to lock it. I take the stairs two at a time, shoving open the dining room door.

I'm not in control, I'm not even thinking.

There is no reason whatsoever that when I see her smile

kindly, shaking her head politely and without a hint of distress and the man in question drops his head and raises his hands, his friends laughing easily ... there's not a reason in the world that this anger should rise inside me. This building fire.

Except that she already told them she was mine.

I heard on the fucking cameras.

He already knew. She fucking told them. Whether or not they believed her isn't my problem.

"Boss." My security's call for me comes just before the sound of cursing and a picked-up pace from the men at my back.

The men are unsuspecting as Braelynn shies back just slightly.

With the skin stretched tight over my knuckles, turning white and blazing with a heat that's untamed, my fist lands against his jaw.

Surprising every one of them. Braelynn gasps, scooting back against a chair and nearly falling. The two men standing gape at me, their hands up as their friend lies lifeless on the floor.

"She said no." I barely get the words out, my chest heaving and my vision turning red.

## Chapter 6

### Braelynn

My eyes are rimmed red and burn with exhaustion, but I can't bring myself to go into the bedroom yet. It's pitch black this late at night and far too quiet. My mind isn't quiet, though. It's running in circles around the night I've just had at The Club. My knee rocks absently as I think about my first day … well, really all I can think about is Declan Cross.

Even when my phone pings, I think it will be him offering me an explanation of what happened. I've never been so close to a fight like that. If you can even call it a fight. That man didn't have a chance in hell. Declan strode in, knocked him out and stormed out as if nothing had happened. I was stunned to say the least, and if security hadn't escorted me out, I would probably still be standing there wondering what the hell had happened.

Checking my phone, it's not Declan.

*Scarlet: Hey, you ...*

I'm curled up on my couch under a knitted blanket I brought from my mother's, and for a moment I consider not answering her. I need to talk to someone, though.

*Braelynn: Hey.*

I just got home a little after 4:00 a.m., and I feel like I barely survived.

*Scarlet: You okay?*

I try to keep telling myself that nothing much even happened, other than the last two minutes. Even if I discounted that, the office meeting with Declan was intimidating to say the least. Declan isn't the boy I remember. I'm sure none of the Cross brothers are the way I remember, but I didn't realize he would be so different. I didn't know he would be so powerful, and so sexy, and ...

*Braelynn: I could be better. I think I'm in over my head.*

My thoughts don't stop. It's like my mind is running faster than I can process. The whole situation escalated before I could stop it. And the waitresses have sex with people in those rooms on the lower floor. It's not just one warning sign, it's a big row of red flags. They scream at me to run away.

*Braelynn: I could not have anticipated tonight.*

Staring down at my phone, I wonder how that's all I have to say. Maybe I'm still overwhelmed by everything.

*Scarlet: It's a lot but it's worth it. Really. It might be rough at first, but I think you pretty much got the full gist of everything all at once.*

I'm dumbstruck at Scarlet's response. *That shit isn't normal.* Rubbing my eyes, I let my head fall back as I cringe at the thought. What happened today does not exist in the world I live in.

Fistfights. Paid sex. Declan Cross.

I think about telling her I'm done. I even type out the text. *Thanks so much for getting me the job, but I can't go back.* I'm in the process of deleting it when Scarlet sends another message.

*Scarlet: I'm sorry I didn't tell you about the red dresses. It's not always a hard and fast rule and I didn't want to freak you out!*

With everything that took place, I can't even be mad about the red dress. Nothing happened.

*Braelynn: It's okay, it just caught me by surprise. A heads-up would have been nice though.*

*Scarlet: I really am sorry. Are you okay? Feeling good about your next shift?*

Maybe I'm overreacting because of the stress and the adrenaline.

*Braelynn: Tonight was a lot.*

I expected a busy night learning the ropes at a new place. I didn't expect Declan Cross. I didn't expect him to get in a fistfight over me. And I definitely didn't expect the red dresses and what comes with them.

*Scarlet: The Club is a lot but ... it pays well. I forgot to ask you how you made out?*

My gaze drifts to my purse, hanging over the staircase to my right. There's at least a grand in cash. I haven't counted yet, but it's far more than I anticipated. It's more than I could have even dreamed, I know that.

The side pocket of my purse is bulging with all the bills inside.

*Braelynn: You were right about the money. I don't think I could get better tips anywhere else in the city.*

*Scarlet: See! I told you! So it's all good? Forgive me for the red dress and let's become rich bitches together!*

Although I huff a small laugh and feel the first touch of relief since I left, I just can't shake how Declan made me feel. I felt sorry for him. Curious about how he'd become that man. And if I'm honest with myself, I felt scared too. Power bows around him in his office and in The Club, and every time he looked at me, he made it clear that I had none.

*Braelynn: I'm good. Declan is intense.*

*Scarlet: Did he hurt you??*

Her question takes me aback, I even flinch at it. Until I remember the punch. Maybe he's ... maybe he's just like that.

*Braelynn: No. Should I be worried that he would?*

*Scarlet: I've never heard of any woman getting hurt. Not in the club and not by him. But what do you mean by intense? That guy? He should have listened when you said no the first time.*

I type then delete. Type then delete. It's frustrating because so much of it is simply how I feel. How do I explain this to her? This overwhelming feeling like something bad is going to happen. Something that leaves me powerless and at the mercy of a man who doesn't seem to know what that word means.

*Braelynn: He didn't hurt me. I just ... I used to know him. Sort of.*

*Scarlet: How?*

*Braelynn: Long story, too much to text.*

I unfold myself from the couch and make my way to the small kitchen. My bare feet pad on the laminate floor.

The layout for the first floor is simple enough. I could walk circles in the townhouse. There's a bathroom and coat closet in the center with their doors on the right. Dining room in the back, hallway on the right with a staircase, living room in the front, and kitchen on the left.

Boxes are lined up in every room. As I wait for leftover pasta to heat in the microwave, I walk through the dining room that doesn't even have a table yet, down the hallway, trailing my fingers along the wall and running over the closet door and then the bathroom door, past the staircase, into the living room as my phone pings. I ignore it and circle back to the kitchen.

My new place is simple, just like the leftover pasta. It's

hardly enough to appease my appetite, but it'll be enough to sleep at least. Opening the fridge door offers a stream of light, and the sight of an empty fridge apart from a bottle of creamer for my coffee.

With a sigh, I shut the door and then consider opening up a cardboard box I know has nonperishables in it. Pushing the hair out of my face, I decide not to do anything else. I need to sleep, not rearrange my kitchen at nearly five in the freaking morning.

Rubbing my eyes, I move without thinking.

The cabinet door opens, and I resign myself to a bedtime ritual I've used countless times in recent years.

I won't do anything that's going to keep me up any longer, but I put water on for tea. Chamomile will calm me down and help me sleep.

With my hands gripping the edge of the counter, I find myself looking out the kitchen window as I try not to think about the day. This lease is for a corner lot on a busy street. It's cheap, though. The building across the street has a yoga studio on the ground level. Through a crack in the curtains I can see the polished wood floor, which takes me right back to gym class in middle school.

To Declan Cross and the first time I spoke to him, well the first time I wanted to. To the man I know is going to keep me up at night.

I can still smell the lemon polish of the floors and hear

the echo of voices in the large gym.

It's crazy how much time has passed, yet how it still feels like yesterday.

So many years ago. Our shoes squeaked on the floor as the teacher herded us out into the sunshine; it must have been late spring or summer, because it was so warm. I dip the tea bag in the hot water, remembering. Declan sat by himself. He had dark circles under his eyes and a haunted look to his face that was there more than it should have been. Even as a kid I knew, but then again, there were whispers about him and his brothers. Everyone knew.

That day in particular, his expression was ragged. I knew his mom had died, and he just wouldn't do what we were supposed to do for class. Jump rope. We were supposed to count the jumps. The smack of the rope hitting the pavement, the chatter around us—it's all there in my mind, just as it was then. And it all means nothing now, just like back then.

I swung the rope over my head and counted. One. Two. Three. Nobody went near him. They were afraid of him, because of his brothers. He was all alone in his hand-me-down clothes. Like mine, because all of my clothes came from my older cousins. He wasn't so different from me.

He was wrecked. He was alone.

It hurt to look at him, so I looked down at the rope. And at my feet on the ground. One. Two. Three. But I couldn't look away from Declan for long. That was the other thing about him. We weren't so different, but I felt this pull to him. A similarity between us. I was afraid of the Cross brothers, just like all of the other kids, but I thought ... if I could talk to him, maybe we'd understand each other.

I stole a glance at him as the rope came over my head and found him looking my way. He stared right at me, as if he'd heard my thoughts.

A shiver ran through my body. He'd caught me.

The rope fell from my hand and I could hardly breathe. He didn't look away and I knew I had to say something. His mother, I remembered. His mother died. "I'm sorry," I whispered, but the sound didn't make it to him. We were too far apart. I hated to see him look so down, but I also knew it was beyond me to fix it. The fact his mother was dead ... it was too much for me. How could I ever help? But I wanted him to know he wasn't alone.

Because being alone is the worst thing there is in the whole world.

A whistle screeched to my right, scaring me and ripping my eyes away from Declan. The coach rattled off statistics about the number of jumps and who'd gotten gold and who'd gotten silver and bronze.

As if I cared and as if any of it mattered.

When I looked back at Declan, he wasn't there anymore.

I turned in a slow circle, looking at all our other classmates, but he was gone.

My phone pings again and snaps me back to the present. With my tea in one hand, I grab my phone in the living room, once again wishing it was Declan, but it's a string of messages from Scarlet.

*Scarlet: Did he hurt you before? Hello? Hey, where did you go? You okay? You sure it's okay?*

*Braelynn: Sorry. Just made some tea for bed. He didn't hurt me, Scarlet, I promise*

*Scarlet: I thought you might have passed out. If he did, you would tell me, right?*

*Braelynn: Of course*

*Braelynn: I just ... there's a difference between being a waitress and doing other things. Not that I'm judging*

*Scarlet: Wear black. Just tell them no. Trust me! The guys that come in know they won't leave alive if they hurt us.*

I don't tell her I already know to wear black. Declan told me as much. Instead I take the phone with me back to the kitchen, back to my tea.

I tip a sleeping pill out of the bottle I keep in the cupboard and wash it down with a sip of hot chamomile. The ceramic clinks on the counter as I stare out of the window again. The roads are empty. I probably shouldn't text her back what I really think, which is that those men standing guard while women sleep with clients is exactly why I'm not sure I can go back. The Club isn't the real world. It's too involved with illegal shit.

The safer thing is to send her back a heart emoji, which I do before heading to the living room.

Then I pull the blanket over my lap, settling back into the sofa, and reach for the TV remote. I've got the TV set up on a little console, but the living room is full of stacks of boxes just like every other room in this place. Not much is unpacked yet, just like the bedroom.

I flick through the channels one after the other. It's a bunch of infomercials and late-night stuff that doesn't catch my attention. It's too hard to tell what's on, and I can't focus anyway, so I turn it off and sip my tea.

My laptop's on the coffee table, plugged into an outlet across the room. It's a long enough cord to pull it into my lap. When I open it, all my old searches are waiting for me in the tabs of my internet browser.

It's just like that day at gym class. I'm looking for him, but I can't find him. There's not much on the internet about Declan Cross or his brothers. If you ask anyone on the street, they could tell you more than what's available online.

The only concrete information that's searchable are the deaths he endured, one after the other. His mother passed while we were in middle school. His brother, Tyler, in high school. Shortly after, his father died. I skim through their obituaries, which are sterile funeral home notices without much of a personal touch. It's as if someone has left these records just so there's something to find. It's weird, in today's day and age, to find nothing but an obituary online, especially for people like the Cross brothers. I run a few more searches. Declan Cross. Carter Cross. Cross brothers and Fallbrooke.

They went from poor kids on the bad side of town to the men who run it, seemingly overnight. My mind reels, wanting to know what happened. What happened to Declan Cross?

*Scarlet: I know it's late, I just hope you know it's good money, and the Cross brothers have helped me before.*

*Scarlet: You know, some men are bad, but others are just bad for bad guys, know what I mean?*

I let her messages sink in before responding and turning back to my laptop.

*Braelynn: I'll sleep on it <3*

There's a long pause. I entertain myself by going back through my searches one more time, even though I know there will be nothing new to find.

The only way I'll find out anything concrete about the Cross brothers—and about Declan—is to go back to The Club for another shift.

I close my laptop, put it in its place on the coffee table, and lean my head back on the couch. The chamomile is kicking in. The sleeping pill too. But my uneasiness doesn't go away.

It's one thing to work at a place that's adjacent to the shady underground of the city. Oh, who am I kidding—it is the underground, if they have sex rooms in the basement. It's another thing to go down there yourself.

And yet that's where Declan Cross has his office. The Club is his world. I feel that same pull to him that I did on the playground all those years ago. It's a dangerous, forbidden curiosity. We're not kids anymore, and I know better than to trust men like him. Especially men with power.

My phone pings again.

*Scarlet: Promise me you'll give it one more chance. Okay? One more shift?*

I hesitate to type out the message. Part of me wants to be easygoing and make the promise. But then ... that's why it took me so long to untangle myself from Travis. And even that's not fully done. If it was, he wouldn't be texting me from new numbers and saying the shit he does. Life, Travis—it's all relentless.

*Braelynn: Sleep well, I'll message you in the morning :)*

There. Not so hard. No promises made. I can sleep on my decision tonight, like a responsible adult. I'll make my decision in my own time without recklessly agreeing to anything.

My head is hazy from the sleeping pill as I go back into the bedroom and tug the corner of the sheet down on the bed. I remember to plug in my phone, which is good, because this pill is well on its way to knocking me out. My head has barely hit the pillow before I can feel myself floating.

I dream of The Club. It's all endless black tablecloths and couples in expensive outfits and an imposing red door. I'm not afraid of the door. I go to it, knowing I'm supposed to be there, and it opens easily, like I've been invited. Chills spread down my body as Declan looks up from his desk. There are no dark circles under his eyes. They're the same stunning shade they always were. His gaze roams down my body and the door closes behind me, trapping me there, with Declan Cross.

# Chapter 7

## Declan

There's faint bruising on the knuckles of my right hand and I run the thumb of my left over it as I watch the show. The dining room is nearly always packed on Thursdays.

Men in my line of work and the everyday patron have a certain addiction in common: sex. The phrase "sex sells" is timeless and there's a reason for that.

The lights are dim, and my gaze moves from the stage to the corner booth of the dining room. All eyes are focused on the two women, bound tight with coarse rope and suspended from the ceiling … all eyes on them save two men in tailored suits.

The deal is almost done and as if on cue, a woman is spun, her back arched, her body covered in striations from the ties of the rope. The audience applauds the demonstration and the two men stand, buttoning their jackets and shaking hands.

Marco's gaze meets mine and with the raise of my tumbler, he gives a short nod.

The crack of the whip behind him causes the man to flinch, and then a grin lifts up the corners of his lips. I watch as his trading partner's shoulders rise and fall with a chuckle. It's good for Davis that Marco is so easygoing and doesn't take any offense to the laughter. Marco turns to face the stage, watching as the woman's skin lights a bright pink from where the leather cat-o'-nine-tails has struck her. Even from this distance, I swear I can hear the soft moans of pleasure spilling from the woman's mouth. Her hair is pulled back tight in a bun, and the stage performer grabs it, tilting her head to devour her lips.

"It won't be long until they're fucking on stage," Mia comments as the glass clinks on the counter. I glance down to see another two fingers of whiskey at the ready for me.

Downing my drink, I slide her the empty one. "I believe that's what most of the audience is waiting for," I respond with a smirk, although it falls as my gaze moves to Braelynn.

She barely watches, just like the rest of the servers. They work diligently, taking care of the guests who are awestruck by the entertainment.

They're not the only ones she avoids.

It's been three days of her staying as far from me as

possible. It's a rare moment when I catch her gaze. More than likely because I've hidden myself away in my office, watching her and looking into her background.

Braelynn Lennox has secrets. Not the least of which is a life she's just run away from, and I'm aware of every sordid detail. I'm all too aware of it.

The black dress clings to her curves as she bends at the waist to collect a stray cocktail napkin that's fallen. A deep, low groan of appreciation leaves me without my conscious consent. My eyes close slowly as I attempt to rid myself of the black lace image. Unfortunately, all I imagine in its place is what lies beneath the delicate fabric.

With the crack of the whip cutting through the perverse vision, I open my eyes and she's right there. A foot from me, the closest she's ever been.

Her shy smile accompanies a quick glance before she reaches past the bar to deliver a drink slip to Mia.

"Boss," she says, greeting me like everyone else. There's a sick coldness that settles at the tip of my tongue, capturing the warm tease I had for her.

Her black nails rap on the bar and she hesitantly peeks up at me. All I can do is stare down at her, noting every delicate detail. Including the faint blush that gathers at her neck, traveling to her cheeks and then higher, moving to her temples as she's caught in my gaze.

"Is everything okay, Declan?" she questions in a whisper.

That deep, low groan is silent this time, and it travels lower, to my hardening cock. That's better, my little pet.

Smirking, I lift the whiskey glass to my lips, sipping before I nod and ask her how her night is going.

"It's something else," she answers, swallowing hard and I don't miss how her gaze drops to my lips before she tears it away, the applause of the audience drawing her attention to the stage.

She's quick to bring her attention back to Mia, who hasn't yet touched Braelynn's slip.

I offer up an observation, testing the tension between us. "Tonight's entertainment is one of the more popular shows."

One look down, and it's evident her nipples are hard. Were they like that when she walked up here? The thin lace can't hide her desire.

She's quiet, only nodding at my commentary. "Are you curious?" I ask her.

Her dark eyes meet mine and this time there's fire. The flames of it consume the oxygen around us. Fuck. What that look does to me is positively sinful. The heated stare doesn't deny the pull between us. I could get lost in that gaze of hers and abandon the boundaries we're toying with altogether. She hesitates at my question, but settles on one of her own. "Curious or scandalized?"

"If that scandalizes you," I start, lifting my drink to the stage, "you may want to reconsider your employment here." It's meant as a joke of sorts, or perhaps a warning but as she glances back at the stage, without her expression easily seen, my body heats with an anxiousness that she could leave. She could so easily walk out of those doors and never come back.

The cords in my neck tighten, but then surprise takes hold of me at her response. "Is that what you like?" she asks in a soft murmur.

Depraved thoughts filter into my mind.

The ice clinks in my glass as I face her and say, "What did you ask?" My tone is deathly low as the background music continues to play, the whip cracks and Braelynn's eyes close, her shoulders shuddering as if the tanned leather strips had stuck against her flesh. I can imagine how her olive skin would brighten, how the rush of fresh blood would be pulled to the surface. How sensitive she'd feel on every inch I played with.

She stares back at me, seemingly unaffected as I imagine her plump lips parted with a strangled cry of pleasure. "Is that what you like?" she asks again, quieter this time, tilting her head in the direction of the stage.

The woman on the stage is wrapped tightly in rope and at Braelynn's question, my eyes easily undress her, imagining her gorgeous tan skin decorated in black satin binds.

"If it crosses a line—"

Rather than answer her, I ask my own question. "Do you

like the idea of being bound?"

"I wouldn't know," she answers and then glances past me, checking on Mia and the state of the drinks I imagine she's waiting on.

"Do you think you'd like to give up control, to be a fuck toy to whatever a man like me would want?" I question her, expecting the phrase *fuck toy* to throw her off. To send her back to the other side of The Club.

It doesn't, though. Her body tenses slightly, her thighs subtly clenching. My grip tightens on the glass as my throat dries. She seems to ponder it and my cock gets impossibly hard. Pulling her bottom lip into her mouth with her teeth, she hums softly before looking back up at me.

Tease. She's nothing but fate's temptation for me.

"Would you want to do it in front of others ... on a stage like them?" she asks and the world pauses around us. Not a sound can be heard. It all blurs as I peer down at her, curiosity evident but so damn innocent.

She has no idea how I'd love to shove my cock down her throat, her hands bound behind her back, that black dress ripped down the front. If I could have her on her knees, struggling to catch her breath as her mascara ran down her face and her eyes brimmed with tears ... I would have her every fucking day just like that.

Every instinct in me wants to drag her back to my office and show her exactly what I'd do to her. If she were my pet, mine to toy with. Mine to do whatever I desire.

"Would you?"

"I don't know... I guess," she answers as I stand impossibly still, not trusting myself. The reminder that she could be undercover and playing me screams in my head. Screams at me that if I wanted, she'd let me, that she'd do it just to get closer to me.

This beautiful, innocent woman would allow me to do every sordid thing I've ever wanted.

"Stop it," I say, pushing out the words and then finish my drink, sucking the whiskey against my teeth.

"What?" She whispers the word with disbelief, taking a step back. I watch her from my periphery as I slam the tumbler down on the bar as gently as I can, although the adrenaline rushes through me, its intensity demanding I let it take over. Without looking at her, listening to the applause, I know not a soul in this room has any idea how on edge I am. What this woman does to me isn't justifiable.

"Don't say another word," I command her and then move my gaze to meet hers. Her dark eyes swirl with a mix of emotion. The cords in her neck tighten as she swallows thickly. "You need to stop before something bad happens to you, Braelynn."

# Chapter 8

## Braelynn

Yesterday's conversation plays back in my mind as I stand here, remembering last night.

The whips and the couple on the stage who performed all manner of sinful deeds for the crowd barely penetrate my consciousness as my body heats. All I can think about is the warning tone from Declan for me to stop.

Swallowing down the memory, I choose to ignore it. Just like I did last night, even if the thought of him doing whatever he'd like to me is exactly what I dreamed of last night. And exactly what I touched myself to this morning. My imagination runs wild with wondering about the things Declan enjoys in the bedroom. I have no right thinking of him like that, but every bit of my intuition begs me to submit to him and let him engage in all manner of depravity. There are whispers about what Declan enjoys.

Clearing my throat, I hover at the bar waiting for Mia to refill the drinks for table six. She does it quickly, her hands working efficiently. It's then I note, Mia always wears black. I wear black now too. Declan's orders, of course. I wonder if he ordered her to as well, or if that's her preference. The question stays in the back of my mind; I wouldn't dare ask her.

It's a slow Wednesday afternoon. Other than Mia, expertly mixing the cocktails, not a soul is in a hurry.

Really slow, actually. There are only four tables occupied. My table is a two-top. Two men in suits, obviously doing business. The two of them were a little heated earlier, their voices rising above the soft music that floats through the room, but they settled down when I came over. They've been quiet and patient since. I can sense they're both making an effort with each other, so I've been hesitant. I don't want to interrupt an important negotiation.

I've learned some clients of The Club are ... particular and handled more delicately than others.

When Mia hands me the drinks, I murmur a quick thank-you. I don't think she even heard it. Her attention is elsewhere and I don't take it as a slight. Something's obviously on her mind, or maybe she's hungover.

I opt to imagine it's the second, and that she'll be her normal self before the dinner rush. With the two drinks, a White Russian and a Tom Collins, balanced on the tray, I take it over to the men and slide it in front of the first one. He nods without stopping the flow of conversation, but the other man interrupts.

"Could we get more," he questions as he brushes the empty white porcelain dish with his fingers. The mix of honey roasted assorted nuts and dried fruits has vanished since the last time I was here. Perhaps that's a good sign.

"Of course," I say and pick up the small bowl without hesitation.

Many men come here to do business. It's been obvious the last few days, and Scarlet said she's noticed too. She also said it's best not to ask questions, or to linger around the tables. At The Club, privacy is a top priority. So I don't stay longer than I have to, and I don't ask questions. Half the time, I don't want to interrupt at all.

Instead, I wonder about The Boss.

That's what everyone calls Declan here. The Boss. Although he didn't seem to like it when I called him it yesterday. A chill runs through me as I work without thinking, dropping the small bowl off, only to be asked for another White Russian.

The man's already downed it.

With a nod and another softly spoken *of course*, I take his tumbler back to the bar.

"Table six again," I tell Mia. She glances down at the

empty glass in my hand.

"One second, Brae, I've got to grab more coffee liqueur from the back."

While she's gone, my attention drifts toward the black door that blends in with the wall. That door leads to Declan. The Boss. The man behind the red door. I'm enthralled with him. There's no better way to put it. Every time I have a moment to myself, I think about him. I try not to, especially when I'm on shift, but I can't stop. The images come fast and furious. Declan leaning against his desk, his dark eyes raking over me. The way he told me not to wear red ... ever again. I think of him constantly at work, and when I lay my head down at night, I dream of him.

With the uncomfortable heat lingering on my skin and the conversation from last night coming back to me, I do everything I can not to recall the way he warned me away ... because it only makes me want him more.

Standing up straight, I place my fingertips on the edge of the bar. The feelings I have for Declan Cross can't be denied. Emotion rushes through me every time I think of him. A different emotion every time, it seems. Right now ... I'm wondering what would have happened if I stayed in his office and stripped for him. After he told me not to wear red ever again, I could have taken the hem of that short dress and pulled it right over my head. What would he have done?

What would *I* have done?

In fact, I think of that very scene most of the time I'm here. Every quiet moment where the black door comes into view. That scenario where I'd stayed and been bold and given into the sordid desire he lights within me.

With my eyes closed, I remember exactly why that's not going to happen.

And then every other little detail that pushes me away comes back full force. All of the warnings and fine print that come when you make a deal with the devil.

That hall downstairs scares me the most. It gives me chills to think about walking down it, and I'm not sure why. The image of that red door does nothing but excite me. The hall, though... the very thought of it causes a chill that elicits a prick of caution, lifting every small hair on the back of my neck.

Scarlet said not to worry about what happens in those rooms downstairs. She said that I'm welcome to go down there if I like. We're all welcome. Then again, I'm not really welcome, am I? Declan said not to wear red, which means I'm not allowed to *engage* with anyone. Even if I want to. I'm still not sure I'd ever want to ... not with any guest. When I think about taking someone down there, I can't picture walking down that hall, or even entering one of the private rooms. All I can think about is Declan's red door.

The sound of Mia clinking the glasses brings me back to the present.

As I gather my composure, she makes the drink I've been

waiting for. I glance over my shoulder, but before I can leave to drop it off, she says, "Braelynn, wait."

"Yeah?"

"After you drop that off, can you head downstairs for me? In the far back room, there's a box of sugar crystals. It says sprinkles on the box but it's not sprinkles." She brushes the hair from her face, seeming even more tired than earlier. "Either way, I need it, and Benji is swamped. I'm trying to help him out. Can you?"

A chill comes over me. Those damn halls are toying with me today, but I smile back at her as if nothing is wrong. Everything's fine. It's just an errand on the lower floor, and nothing more. "Of course I will. Need anything else while I'm down there?"

"That's it. Thank you." She stresses her gratitude, taking in a long breath and letting out an even longer exhale before heading back behind the bar. Maybe the kitchen is short-staffed, I'm not sure, but I can grab a box from downstairs easily enough. It's not like we're busy.

With the tray in hand, I deliver the drink to the businessman at my table.

They're both stiff and quiet, staring at each other. It's tense. My simper is plastered on as if I can't tell. As if it's not suffocating being within ten feet of them. If I had to guess, the negotiations aren't going well. "Do you two need anything else?" My voice is too bright, a little too loud, but it seems to shake them out of it. The mood lightens slightly as I stand at the side of the table, the tray tucked under my arm.

One of them smiles and laughs a little, sipping at his drink.

The other, the man who's downed his White Russians without taking time to taste them, slides his hand onto the small of my back. "Maybe some ..."

My spine stiffens and without my conscious consent, my gaze is ripped away to the black door. As I take a small step back, the man blinks, seeming to take in my dress for the first time. He yanks his hand away like I burned him. "I didn't mean any disrespect."

"It's okay," I reassure him, although everything in me is on high alert.

His hand barely touched me, but it was more than obvious and I know Declan watches. The last thing I need is for Declan to be upset. I don't know exactly what happened the first night, what set him off, but I don't want that again. I wonder if the man knows what happened the other night. "My apologies, sincerely."

"It's fine, really." I play it off and swallow down any fear. The color has already drained from the man's face. It's even more obvious because of his dark suit. Both men seated at the table are dressed in what appear to be expensive suits, custom tailored to their frames, but both men are rough around the edges. There's nothing smooth or charming or ... well-bred about them. They're gangsters, is what they are.

"Is there anything else I can get for you?"

"No. You're perfect," the second one says. Now he's making a point to smile at me, leaning back in his chair to put space between us. "We're all good."

With the anxious bundle in the pit of my stomach, I flee to the black door.

I head down to get the sprinkles. Down those hard iron stairs. At the bottom I pause and take stock of my options. There's Declan's red door, down one part of the hall, but which room is the back room?

Fuck. My head's a mess and I didn't bother to ask which room is which. The last thing I want is to open the wrong door. I should have asked Mia for specific directions. Not that anyone is here, I remind myself.

It's not like I'm going to walk in on anyone. Ridding my clouded head of the apprehension, I pick the first door I come to. I'll find the damn back room myself.

It's dark when I open it, and I reach inside, fiddling for a light. The second it snaps on, I know it's not the right room.

My eyes widen and my lungs still.

This is one of the sex dens. I've never seen a room with so much red silk inside it. The room smells fresh and new, but everything is elegant, luxurious and red, red, red. And perfect.

Not a single thing is out of place. It's an invitation for sin and indulgence. My gaze moves from piece to piece, imagining what goes on in each corner of the room.

I'm breathless with the shock of it. I knew the rooms were down here. I didn't think seeing them would have an effect on me. It's not like I've never seen a four-poster dark wood bed before. Apparently, the cuffs attached to them have more of a hold on me than I thought something like this would.

Suddenly, a hand on my back startles me. It's firm. Possessive. Hot, like fire.

Gasping, I'm quick to move away from it.

"Braelynn." My name is spoken lowly, and shivers run all through my body. Declan's close. The closest he's ever been. "Did someone say you could come down here?" The deep rumble of his voice holds a playful note to it. He's teasing me, I think, and I'm torn between a mixture of fear and desire, and the urge to laugh and break the tension.

"I'm just looking for sprinkles," I say and swallow, forcing myself to look at him. He arches a brow. "Not sprinkles. Sugar crystals for Mia. For the bar." I take another step back and another steadying breath. "For drinks."

Declan's gaze doesn't leave mine, but I can feel the clothes peeling away from my skin. I can feel his eyes on the curves under my dress as if I'm naked in front of him. Like he's undressing me with the force of his dark eyes alone.

"The back room is at the other end, down the other hall," he says. "There's nothing to the left of my office, unless this is what you're after." Heat flushes over my face and everywhere else. With another deep breath, I do everything I can to remain professional.

Declan isn't trying, though.

In his sharp suit and a deep red tie, he's the very essence of professional ... yet somehow he could occupy the title of sex god at the very same time.

His gaze slips down to my nipples, which are hard through my dress. This dress doesn't allow for a bra, so I didn't wear one. He knows now. He knows everything. "Is this what you're after, Braelynn? You came to play rather than work?"

"No, Declan." I step aside, my sights focused on remaining professional. He barely moves, so my skin brushes his sleeve as I go. His footsteps follow me down the hall.

With every hard thump behind me and within my chest, all I can imagine are the two of us in that room. In my fantasy I'm bound and he does whatever he wants to me.

"Didn't your friend tell you not to come down here?" he questions. His voice is so deep and rough. Every time he speaks it goes right to my core. "Scarlet."

"No."

"Are you two not close then?"

"No, we're—we're close. I've known her for about three years now." My mind spins back through all the history I've shared with Scarlet. It doesn't seem possible for it to have been three years already, but it is. I'm barely thinking when I answer, "She was a good friend to me when my father died."

"Your father passed?" His tone completely changes with

those words. I hear the sympathy in his voice, and it surprises me. It changes everything. The atmosphere, the tension. It's as if his concern has washed away all else. Stopping where I am just outside his red door and nearly back at the winding iron staircase, he tells me in a murmur, "I'm sorry to hear that." Glancing up and over my shoulder, I look into his eyes to find sincerity there too.

"Thank you." Something between us pulls tight, so that I almost lean into him. I would like that, I think. To lean into his strong body and let him hold me up for a minute. His hands move to his tie, tucking it beneath his jacket and for a moment, he isn't the intimidating man who taunts me, who tempts me. He's that boy in school I knew was hurting and I desperately wanted to know.

"It's this way, Braelynn." He tilts his head and repositions himself so he's leading the way.

"Right," I whisper although he doesn't wait for me. I follow him as we go down the hall, and Declan gestures to a room.

"Oh, wow." Embarrassment stains my cheeks and I feel about two inches tall. The door is literally labeled "Back room."

Declan makes a sound that could be a laugh. "Your friend Scarlet didn't show you the back room?"

"No, she didn't."

"So she wants you to get into trouble. Is that it?"

"No." She doesn't want me to get into trouble. Scarlet is the person who wants me to keep this job the most, I think.

Without her I may never have come back for day two. "Mia's the one who asked me to come down here; Scarlet isn't in yet."

He nods, his hands slipping into his pockets. "Understood."

It would be the end of the conversation, but Declan's eyes stay on me, and after a minute I can't look away. He's intoxicating. It makes me nervous as hell when he does this, but it also makes my heart pound with excitement.

He tears his eyes from me and opens the door to the back room. "Go in and get your sugar crystals." Just like that, it's ended.

It was a direct order, so I enter the room, my knees still trembling and my mind still getting a grip on everything that's happened. Mia said the box would be labeled with sprinkles, so that's what I look for. Large shelves hold many, many boxes of supplies for the bar and the restaurant. All things that can be safely stored down here. Declan's eyes are on me the entire time. I find the box easily enough and pull it off the shelves. If he comes in here and closes the door behind us, then this is the beginning of one of the many fantasies I've had about him.

He doesn't come in and every minute that passes I scold myself for thinking he would. He keeps a professional distance.

I start to think it's all in my head.

He waits until I'm taking a step into the hall, and then his large hand wraps around my arm. The box drops to the floor as I gasp. It doesn't open as it crashes beneath us and he pulls me closer to him. Everything blurs as his face comes into view, his eyes piercing mine.

He controls every aspect, pinning me against the wall with my hand above my head. He leans in close, the warmth of his breath on my ear. "I'm warning you, Braelynn. If this is too much for you, you should walk away, because there's so much more than this." My eyes close. Everything he said should terrify me, but all I want is for him to stop warning me. His heated breath tickles along the crook of my neck as he whispers there, "If you don't want to do this, walk away."

With his thigh between my spread legs, goosebumps erupt over my skin. Both of us are still as my hammering heart calms, his hard body pressed to mine. It's only when he loosens his grip slightly and pulls back that I turn my head to look into his eyes, the eyes that see through me, the eyes that I can't look away from. *If you don't want to do this, walk away.*

I plant my feet and stay where I am, even when he lets go of me completely.

Declan stares back at me, waiting. One second passes. Two seconds and the world between us is set on fire.

I think he leans in first, but it could be me. Our lips crash in a devouring kiss. Almost as if he's pissed off I came down here, and almost as if I'm pissed off that he's frustrated he can't keep me down here. Neither thing can be true. I want this too much.

Declan breaks the kiss so abruptly I gasp in a breath. I'm still trying to catch it when he opens his red door and disappears behind it again, leaving me alone in the hall, reeling and uncertain, with the tips of my fingers at my lips.

# Chapter 9

## Declan

She's touched her lips three times already tonight. As I stare at the screen, watching Braelynn gripping the end of the bar and absently staring at the lined glass bottles accentuated by the bar's dim light, apprehension consumes me. Until those slim fingers lift up and she does it again.

Every time she stops at the bar, when time waits quietly and she's still, her thumb brushes her lower lip as she stares at the marble bar top. If that wasn't enough of an indication she's thinking of me, her gaze shifts to where I stood beside her a few nights ago. Throughout the evening, every time she's stopped moving, I'm almost certain she's thought of me. She wants this, maybe as much as I do.

There are a million reasons I shouldn't have kissed her. Zero reasons I should have. Except for the fact that I wanted to.

My blood chills as I lean back in the chair and she leaves the bar, the tray filled with martini glasses. If she's undercover, if she's working for the feds, or even just an informant ... what I'm about to do could not only destroy me, but also my brothers. Thoughts of my nieces and nephews I've barely seen flicker through my mind. My entire family could go down if I don't figure out who's been passing the feds information.

With a grim outlook my gaze turns from the screen, just in time for an email to come through. It's from a throwaway address.

*There's nothing that says she should be the one who's undercover.*

The single subject line doesn't hold any text in the body of the email. But there is an attachment. I filter through the background check and other documents he discovered, most of which I've come to learn this past week.

There's nothing that hints at her being involved, but she is friends with Scarlet. Given that her father passed and Scarlet was there for her, they're closer than I first anticipated.

The knock at my door precedes it opening and I don't have to look to know it's my brother.

"You might want to get in on this," he says. Jase's tone is somber and it captures my attention. He nods slightly when my questioning gaze meets his.

"Scarlet is only one of them."

Pushing the chair back from my desk, I stand up, buttoning my suit jacket as if it has any place in what's about to happen. My pace is swift and Jase follows behind me as I stride out of my office. The door closes and I lock it before heading down the hall. All the while my body slowly numbs.

She's only one of them. There are more for certain.

Swallowing thickly, I ready myself. This isn't the first time or even the hundredth I've done this and yet each time, there's a heaviness that weighs down every step.

My heart seems to slow, as does time.

"What else did he say?" I question just beneath my breath as my brother leads me to the back room.

The music from upstairs is loud tonight, and that's by design. The door opens with an eerie groan and I'm quick to close it and lock it behind me before I follow Jase around to the back where a shelf is moved aside. A hidden door leading to a soundproof chamber opens with a gentle push on a disguised lock.

My pulse races, fresh adrenaline coursing through my blood. The stench of piss is the first thing to hit me under the fluorescent lights. The man's jaw cracks as Seth's fist slams against it and blood sprays from his lip.

The man's head sways, his hands bound behind his back in the bolted-down chair.

Many men have rushed secrets out of busted mouths in this room.

As Jase pulls a chair closer to him, to continue his interrogation, Seth steps back. His shirt is stained with blood, as are his worn jeans.

"How long has it been?" I ask him. Other than my brothers, he's the closest approximation to a friend I have.

"Going on three," he answers, his voice even and the man of the hour wouldn't know it, but behind Seth's gaze is a tiredness as well as concern.

"I'm telling you," the man starts, before spitting up blood, "I don't know who." He heaves in a breath, his head still dangling. Jase lifts the man's chin up to look in his eyes. Both are swollen, while one brow sports a gash, and the other is swollen shut.

"I'm sure there's something you can tell us," Jase suggests, tilting his head and urging the man to give up a name or any information that could help us uncover the rat in our midst.

A heat rushes through me as the man heaves in a sob. He knows damn well he'll die here, if not tonight, then early morning. It's pathetic and it speaks to a side of me I long thought was dead.

"I don't know, I swear," he says and with Jase's hand dropping, he leans back as Seth moves in. The man's cheekbone crushes beneath Seth's fist, and his head whips to the side with a vicious crack. For a moment I wonder if Seth broke his neck.

The agony in the man's strangled cry promises me he's

still alive. He wails and his pain ricochets off the walls of this concrete chamber. Other than three simple steel chairs, one bolted to the floor in the center of the room, there's nothing else here in the hidden back room.

"I don't know." The man's inhale is harsh and sudden. The clot of blood he coughs up forces Seth and Jase to exchange a glance. It won't be long. This informant won't last another hour. "They didn't share the names," he confesses, his eyes closed, his head hung heavy.

I move in, gripping his chin and staring down into his very soul.

"How many?" I question.

"Two." His answer is immediate.

"Both here?" He nods, a useless, weak nod I barely feel against my hand.

"How long?" I ask and he answers, "For years."

It's my only consolation as I back away, wiping the blood from my palm on the man's jeans.

In a white shirt with a nondescript logo, faded jeans and brown boots, I imagine this isn't what he wanted to die in.

"How did you find him?" I ask Jase, although I don't turn to my brother. I keep my focus on the man we're minutes from murdering.

As my brother tells me, his answer fades into the background. Everything in this moment takes me back to years ago. Back to when I first knew our lives weren't like everyone else's. There was something wrong with us, but we would survive if we had each other.

Braelynn was there, in this memory. As Seth resumes his onslaught, as Jase screams for answers and barters lies for truth, I remember a moment with her as I left school. I knew whatever I was leaving for was something that would haunt me. I stayed after school to watch the football team practice. I'd been thinking of trying out. Really, though, I stayed to watch Braelynn working with the athletic trainers. But Jase texted me he was there; that they needed me.

As I walked down the front steps, I felt her eyes on me. It was like she knew. Like she wanted to stop me. She didn't, though. No one ever did.

Carter was in the back of Jase's car, his face much like the man's tonight. The smell of alcohol was apparent, but I knew it didn't come from my brother. My father was the only one Carter would allow to beat him like that.

I remember how loud it was when I swallowed. How Jase had to grip my shoulders to get my attention and keep me from staring at Carter.

"Everything's all right, I just ... I need you to drive." He was nodding his head before I could answer. "Can you do that?"

"Where are we going?"

"To the water," Carter answered, his tone dull, but he patted the back of the driver's seat with a welcoming gesture. It was a rare day where I felt genuinely needed.

For most of my life, I'd been the kid crying, the kid who was in the way. "Get in."

When we were halfway there, Jase and Carter discussed how long it would take to dig. There was a hill at the dock; it led up to thick woods on the left and a dense field on the right. "We'll bury him by the field. It'll be spring before they even find his body."

That was the first moment I heard them say it out loud. There were so many things we never said out loud. We didn't talk about how we missed our mother. We didn't talk about how hungry we were or how fucked the house was with all the repairs it needed. We didn't talk about how Dad was killing himself with alcohol. And how he took out his anger on my oldest two brothers.

We sure as hell didn't talk about the drugs. Or the rumors that Carter had killed people. They were bad men. That's what I told myself. But as I drove the two hours to the docks, and the night got darker, they talked about burying the man in the trunk.

I remember watching them as the sun nestled behind the woods, their shadows took over the night and the thudding sounds of the violated dirt buried their way into my memory.

I'll never forget that evening.

"Why did you need me to drive?" I asked Jase as Carter finished up in the distance.

"Adrenaline is ..." Jase trailed off and sniffled, the cold of the night turning his nose a dark pink. He looked me in the eyes and said, "Adrenaline was high."

I knew it was a lie and took a stab at the truth, saying, "You didn't want me to go home to him." We'd never said a number of things out loud before that night, but after it was over, there were no more secrets to keep.

"That too." Jase's eyes were clouded with sorrow.

"You can tell him." Carter spoke up from behind me before swinging the shovel into the rear of the hatchback.

"Someone started something and—" Jase began and I cut him off.

"That's real specific."

"He said he was going to kill the Cross brothers."

Carter added, "All of us," before shutting the trunk with a loud clank. The car jostled with the harsh shove.

"Life might be fucked," Jase said and met my gaze. "But we'll never leave you behind. All right?"

"I'm going to take care of it. I'll fix it," Carter said and gripped my shoulder, squeezing it as his voice got tight with emotion. He was barely twenty-five and we'd just lost Tyler. "I'm going to fix it."

"When's Daniel coming home?" I asked them because at that moment, I swore I'd lose them one by one. I felt it in my bones. We were all going to die. I just didn't realize the kind of deaths men like us have.

Carter answered, "I told him to stay away for now."

Jase added, "He'll be home after getting something. We're waiting to hear back from a man named Marcus."

The last bit of the kid I was died that night when I asked, "Are we going to be okay?"

"Always. It doesn't matter what happens, all right? I told you, I'll take care of it and you'll be all right. I'll kill every last one of them before anyone hurts you."

# Chapter 10

## Braelynn

The outside patio at the pub is the perfect place to be on my day off. It's brisk, but not cold. Especially with the sun shining down, giving a hint of warmth. It's quiet and a piece of normalcy. There's no place I've ever been that holds the same atmosphere as The Club. Being here is like coming back to reality. And heaven knows I need that after last night.

Taking a sip of the cider, I try not to think of last night. Of the kiss. Of him leaving me and not coming back up to see me.

I have no idea what we are or what we're doing. It's another piece of that prominent enigma that is Declan Cross. His life, his club, his touch ... they're unfathomable for a woman like me. And yet here I am, caught in his trap.

"Refill?" the waitress asks just as I bottom out the cider. She's quick to bring me another, and all the while I focus on anything other than Declan.

I've always loved the early fall when the breeze is still gentle but the air is crisp. I hold a heavy glass of chilled apple cider in one hand and my phone in the other. My stomach turns. Everything was perfect until the message came in. Now my heart beats faster with anxiety. The patio feels too exposed now. There's no door to lock between me and the rest of the world. I glance at the message one more time as if looking back down would change what I saw.

*Travis: You need to call me back. I deserve a damn response from you.*

My throat goes tight, partly with fear but also with anger. He's so damn entitled. Gritting my teeth, I set the phone down and take a longer sip of the cider, wishing it was spiked. Hell, I'd even take whiskey just to have the edge softened. I don't owe my ex-husband a damn thing. He doesn't deserve anything from me, not after all he's taken.

Yet the level of anger doesn't rise to where it should. I should be furious, and instead I'm irritated and, if I'm honest, a little scared.

Because all I keep thinking about is the kiss.

Travis means nothing. His empty threats mean nothing when Declan Cross just kissed me. It was a kiss that heated me up inside like a fire in the middle of winter. It felt familiar, in a way, but also entirely new. A bit dangerous. A lot forbidden. And then he walked away, almost daring me to follow him. If I had followed him, anything could have happened.

"Everything okay?" my mom asks, startling me and bringing me back to the present as she retakes the seat across from me. The iron legs of the chair scrape on the paved patio as she pushes her chair back in. I trace the pattern on the iron patio table. My phone vibrates and the sound echoes through the metal.

The smile I force my lips into is a farce. We came before the dinner rush, so there's practically no one else here. "Yeah, everything's good." My mother doesn't need to deal with this mess. It's mine to clean up. So I do everything I can to appease the worry in her gaze.

I take a casual glance at my phone, expecting to see something worse from Travis. The number on the screen isn't his, though. It's a number I don't have saved in my phone.

*Unknown: This is Mr. Cross's associate. If you come in, you'll be working exclusively for Mr. Cross from now on. I realize this is an occupational change that is unexpected. If you'd rather resign, please let me know.*

*Holy fuck.* What? My head spins as I sit across from my mother, attempting to hide every reaction. I don't know what to think. Blinking rapidly, and surrounded by nothing but fresh air, it's still nearly impossible to catch my breath. My heart hammers as I reread the message, making sure I understand exactly what the hell is happening. Working exclusively for Mr. Cross. Is it because I couldn't cut it as a waitress, or ... because of that kiss?

*If you'd rather resign ...* That doesn't sit well with me. Instantly, I'm on high alert.

"The blood just drained from your face, *nena*. What is going on?" My mother's dark eyes meet mine from across the table. With wide eyes I stare back at her. I've never been able to hide a thing from my mother.

It doesn't seem prudent to mention the Cross brothers, though. It does feel like lying, but she doesn't need to know. She'll worry herself to death. Especially when I don't have the first clue what this is about. I turn my phone over so the screen doesn't show.

"Travis has been messaging me." I offer up the alternative truth. It's a relief to be honest with her and it makes my heart sink to omit any part of it.

She curses under her breath in Spanish, sweeps her napkin up from the table, then throws it back down. The wrinkles around my mother's eyes show her age but also her worry. I hate that look on her. It kills a part of me that knows I'd be in a better place in my life if only I'd listened to her years ago.

"No, Mama, it's okay." I'm quick to reach across the table and grab her hand. "Really. It's okay." With my hand over hers I stress, "I can handle it."

Her bottom lip drops as if she'll say something, but

she decides against whatever it was. Instead, she shakes her head, her short bob swaying with the movement. "I'm telling your uncle."

Her stern voice sets off that same response it has since I was a child.

My words are rushed when I tell her, "Don't do that. No one needs to get involved." Pulling her hand away, she shakes her head again, staring down at her cup of tea that's most certainly gone cold now.

"He needs to leave you alone." Her voice goes breathless when she says it, and my heart breaks.

"Mama."

She doesn't want me to be hurt. She wasn't convinced that me moving out of her house was the best idea, but I had to do it. I'm twenty-five. I need to move on. I had to make something of myself. I couldn't hide in her house forever.

"Can we eat? Please? Our food will be here any second. I'll block his number." *Again.* She doesn't know I've already blocked it before. And she doesn't need to know either.

It's always going to be "again" with Travis, isn't it? He'll keep pushing, demanding, attempting to control me and hold on to whatever part of my life he can. He'll always be an asshole and I'll keep blocking him, because what else can I do? Over and over until he finally loses interest and lets me get on with my life.

"If anything worries me, if he says anything else or ... or

tries anything else, I will tell you."

Another text comes in. We both avoid looking at the phone for as long as we can, but finally Mama sighs. "Is that him?"

She takes her hand back and watches as I pick up the phone.

"No. It's not him. It's my friend from work. The one who got me the job." Mama knows of Scarlet, but she's only met her a time or two.

"Does she know about Travis?"

*Scarlet: OMG! I just heard you're being moved to personal assistant ... he must really like you!!*

"She knows about Travis," I tell my mom. She knows everything. Scarlet's known me long enough to understand why I needed a job and to be financially independent. Scarlet knows why I have to get my feet under me and make my own life ... far away from my ex.

Scarlet also knows about the kiss last night and how torn I am about everything.

I scroll back through the texts, feeling ... so damn conflicted.

*Braelynn: I did something I shouldn't have.*
*Scarlet: Tell me now. Whatever it is, I'll fix it. It'll be okay.*
*Braelynn: I don't think you can fix this. I kissed Declan.*

I remember how my heart raced after I sent that text and how it took Scarlet forever to respond. It would say she was typing, then it would disappear. Typing. Then nothing.

*Braelynn: Say something! Please!*

*Scarlet: I'm just a little shocked. What are you thinking? Feeling? Tell me everything! Was it good?*

*Braelynn: Your last question has me cracking up. YES! It was good. It was also shocking for me.*

*Scarlet: So you kissed him and you liked it ... did he mention anything after?*

*Braelynn: Not after. Before he said if I didn't want to do it, I should walk away. But ... I really wanted to kiss him.*

*Scarlet: So he didn't say ANYTHING after?? He had to say SOMETHING*

*Braelynn: Nothing ... I went back to work and waited for him to come back up and he didn't, so I just ... I left.*

*Scarlet: I'm just going to say it. I heard he is freaky like BDSM freaky. AND I KNOW - you are curious. I KNOW YOU ARE!*

That was last night after everything happened. And now she's texting me congrats on a new position? Like, it doesn't have anything to do with the kiss ...

That makes the timing of this text feel off to me. It hasn't been two minutes since I got the text myself. Everything feels uneasy. She wasn't honest about the dress colors, and waited far too long to tell me about the rooms downstairs.

I'm so tempted to tell her I'm going to resign. But I know she'll push me to stay. Maybe I'm just looking too much into it.

Declan Cross scares me, but I am curious. I want *him*.

I'm attracted to him, but that doesn't make him or the idea of being with him any less intimidating. And she damn well knows that.

Turning the phone back over, I smile at my mom.

"We're here to have a good lunch," I tell her with an upbeat tone. *Not to get a million texts and make potentially life-changing decisions before the food has even arrived.*

"You can message her back, you know, nena."

I sure can, but knowing Scarlet it will turn into more questioning and more pushing. She's been a good friend to me, but I don't need a long conversation right now or any pressure.

"I just want to have lunch with you. Forget the texts." I wave my hands over the table like I can brush all this away. "What's going on with you?"

My mother purses her lips, and I can tell she's trying to decide if she wants to tell me something. But she'll give in. She always does. "Your uncle's not feeling well."

"No?" I know Uncle Gael has had problems with his hip recently, but I haven't heard anything about that in weeks.

"And ..." This is the part she was hesitating to tell me before. "Travis went to go see him. I don't like that he does that."

"I don't either." Ice spreads through my veins. Visiting my family crosses a line, and Travis doesn't care. He's never given a damn about boundaries. With a steadying breath, I try not to let my anger ruin lunch.

My gaze lifts to the waitress, who's seating another table. As I lift the cider to my lips, I debate asking her to spike it on the next refill.

"Uncle Gael told him he needs to leave you alone and stay away."

As I'm nodding, the food is served.

The two plates are delivered by a different server, a smiling waitress with her dark hair in a ponytail that swings around.

"Thanks," our waitress murmurs to the first and comes up behind her with a side plate of salad for Mama. It's an easy lunch of our favorites. Nearly every time we come here my mother gets the chicken wrap and salad, and I get the same as well. Today I felt like ordering something different, though. Looking down at my Monte Cristo, my mouth waters.

With another tea ordered for my mother and a round of "enjoy," we're left alone again. This time at least there are salty fries that can join my salty attitude toward Travis. I chomp down on one and notice my mother's demeanor. This past year has been hard on her. It's starting to show.

"What's done is done, Mama. Can we talk about something else? Something easy." Smoothing the napkin in my lap, I try not to feel guilty for adding stress to my mother's life.

She unwraps her fork and puts her napkin in her lap. "Something easy," she repeats, thinking. "How is your new job?"

My face flushes. I can't think of my job without thinking of Declan. I think of him constantly. Retreating behind my cider, I give myself a moment before responding.

I think of the heat in his eyes while that demonstration was happening on Thursday night. He wouldn't answer me when I asked him if that was what he liked—the whips and the ropes. Pain and pleasure. He didn't have to answer for me to see the truth. I was honest with him too. I don't know if I would want things to be so ... public. It seems dirty to even imagine, but I can't help it. I have imagined it.

That's what makes the kiss so complicated. It's not just a kiss, it's an invitation. I have some idea of what might have happened if I'd followed him last night, and not retreated back upstairs. He's not a man with vanilla tastes. *You need to stop before something bad happens to you, Braelynn.*

Bad as in ... getting whipped? Bad as in getting hurt? Plenty of bad things have happened to me in my life, but the women on that stage didn't seem to think it was bad.

And if I know anything about Declan's club, it's that they gave consent. No one goes down to the lower floor if they don't want to. No one would be up on that stage if they didn't want to be there.

Or maybe he just meant that if I kept tempting him, I'd end up with him.

My glass clunks as I set it down on the iron a little too hard. "It's going well. I barely ever have a chance to sit, it's so busy."

"I'd like to come visit you at work," my mom mentions.

That stops my imagination in its tracks. "Oh, I don't know, Mama."

"What?" She laughs, her eyes lighting up. "I thought you were a waitress. You can help me find something on the menu to order, right?"

"It's a nightclub." I lift a brow and shrug, hoping she'll understand. "My dresses are a little short."

And depending on when my mother came to visit ... I don't want to have to explain why some of the women are wearing red, and for what. She's observant. She'd notice.

She reaches for my hand and pats it. "Well, you know I don't judge. If it makes you happy, then I'll support you." Her little smirk tells me she knows more than I think she knows.

I head off whatever she's thinking and say, "It's not for better tips."

"I've been around the block a time or two, you know."

"Mama," I say with a gasp and a smile lights up my face. As she chuckles, I join her.

"You do what you have to do. A little skin, a little flirting for a better tip. I get it." She talks as she eats her salad. "You know your grandmother was a waitress all her life."

"I didn't know that."

My mother nods and says, "She got me my first job as a waitress in the cafe."

As my mother tells me stories I've never heard about my abuela, my mind drifts.

It goes straight back to Declan.

How his lips tasted. How his body felt against mine. The rumble of his voice when he whispered at the shell of my ear.

He's not a boy anymore, and I felt a certain amount of fear at being downstairs with him. And ... I wanted it. I know how risky it is to be involved with any of the Cross brothers. They're dangerous men and powerful here in the city. I would never want to go up against them, never want to give them a reason to think negatively of me. What I want is deeper than that, I think. The memory of Declan kissing me is enough to send heat rushing to my cheeks and warmth all through me.

I haven't felt like this since I can remember.

# Chapter 11

## Declan

Scrolling through my phone, I click over to the messages from this morning.

*Declan: I'm delighted to hear you didn't resign.*
*Braelynn: Declan?*
*Declan: Yes. Come to my office when you get here.*

My thumb taps impatiently on the edge of my phone. Last night sealed her fate. I'll be keeping her close. As close as she'd like to get. If that's her intention, to spy on me for Scarlet, or to dig around, there's only one way to know.

My gaze moves to the time. 1:01. Just as irritation grows from the fact that she's already late, there's a knock on the office door. It's firm, and comes in a quick set of three.

*Knock, knock, knock.*

"Come in," I answer, my body tightening. Everything feels tense and every muscle coiled.

The way I'm going to play with this woman, to tease her and use her ... I barely fucking slept last night. My cock's already hard as the door opens and her small frame is shown.

Her ruched black dress hugs her curves and the hem climbs up her thighs with each step, proving she pulled it down before entering. The V-neck isn't deep, but her small breasts still manage to steal the show.

As my gaze roams up her body, I note the shade of red on her lips and how her hair lays perfectly across her shoulders in relaxed curves. She's like a doll, a pretty little thing to play with.

A gorgeous woman to fuck into my ravaged rag doll.

Pushing my chair out a foot, I lean back in my chair and tell her to close the door.

"Declan." My name comes out in a single breath and there's obvious hesitancy.

*Fuck.*

"Yes?" I question as heat engulfs my body.

Her fingers nervously grip one another as she takes a step and then another toward me, but doesn't stride to the desk. Instead she stands awkwardly in the middle of the office.

I'd feel like a prick for doing this to her, if I wasn't questioning whether or not she's conspiring against me with Scarlet.

And if I didn't think she'd love what I'm about to do to her. Informant or not, she can't hide that she's attracted to me. Every little dirty thought is written on her face.

Licking her bottom lip, she takes another step closer.

I grip the armrest to keep me still as she talks.

"I need to know what this is. What exactly is a personal assistant for you?"

The corners of my lips lift into an asymmetric smile. "I need someone to balance the books," I tell her easily enough and the moment her shoulders lower with relief I add, "and I'd like to fuck you. Thoroughly."

A touch of shock hits her gorgeous dark brown eyes and her lips part with a quick intake of breath. My cock aches that much more. "I'd like to play with you and play with whatever this tension is between us."

"Oh," she answers, blinking once and seeming to take it all in with a sharp rise of her shoulders.

"I want you to be my secretary." I take in a steadying breath and then lean forward, my elbows on my knees. "And my fuck toy."

"I see," she whispers, her gaze caught in mine. Turmoil and intrigue war with each other.

"Does that suit you?" I anticipate her hesitating, her wanting time to think perhaps.

Every nerve ending in my body is delighted from her murmured and immediate response. "Yes."

As I lean back in my chair, I decide finances can wait until tomorrow. "Strip."

"Am I—" she starts to question and her eyes flicker with every thought that passes by.

My answering command lacks patience. "Now."

There's a thud in my chest and then another as the seconds pass and Braelynn seems paralyzed where she stands.

It's obvious that she's intimidated, hesitant, possibly scared, but with a heavy breath that drops her chest, forcing my gaze there, she does as she's told.

She may seem afraid, but this deep primal need that forces me to flex my hands as I stay as still as can be fucking terrifies me. I want her more than I've wanted anything in a long time. Maybe ever. With her lips parted, her breaths are slow and steady as the sleeve is stripped from her arm.

"Slowly," I murmur before clearing my throat and readjusting in the chair. Her dark eyes are wide as she stares back at me, one sleeve hanging off the dress, the other nearly removed as well. "I want you to take your time."

She nods although to be fair, there isn't much for her to remove.

"My heels?" She finally speaks and her comment is meant to be teasing and sultry. I'll be damned if she didn't hit her mark as the light kisses her bare skin and the dress is pushed to the floor as she shimmies it off.

"Keep them on."

Leaving her wearing nothing but a simple lace thong and matching bra.

"Have I already scandalized you?" I question and her eyes pierce through me, holding me in place as she reaches behind her. With a quick snap, her bra falls to the floor.

Her breasts are small, a handful maybe, and her nipples beg to be licked. They're soft and I want nothing more than to pluck them, nip them, and suck them until they're hardened peaks. The sight of her bending to remove the last garment is my undoing. As I stand, she pauses.

With a cock of my brow, she continues. Stripping down bare for me, and stepping out of the lace puddle at her feet with the click of her heels on the hardwood floor.

She's utterly breathtaking.

Standing at the edge of my desk, I tap it once. Only once and she obeys the unspoken command.

The lights are dim, but provide plenty of illumination to enjoy the sight before me. Her questioning gaze searches mine and I take her hands one at a time, laying them flat on the desk and slide them across it, pushing the papers to the other end, until her hips are pushed against it and her chest is nearly flat against the desktop.

Moving my hands up her arms, I revel in the shiver that runs through her body and how heavy her eyelids seem to go.

Her breathing picks up, heavier and louder as I trail down her back and then lower, crouching beside her and only stopping to take a handful of her ass and squeeze before laying a heavy slap against her heated skin. Her gasp fuels me as her heels teeter and then she corrects herself.

"Good girl," I murmur against her skin.

She's thicker at her ass and thighs and I lean forward with an openmouthed kiss, noting how her thighs tighten. My hand drifts up the back of her thighs until my fingers slip against her slit. Biting down gently, I listen for her moans, which she gives me easily.

Even her cunt responds, clenching around nothing, although I feel it against my fingers.

A satisfied groan leaves me as I stand, not fully though—I stay bent to spread her pussy lips and give her a languid lick, tasting her sweet arousal. In my periphery, I see her watching and I make sure my desire and contentment are evident as I lick my lips and go in for another taste.

With a quiet mewl she struggles to stay still and my right hand comes down hard on her ass as I command her, "Stay still."

Fuck, the way she groans after that short, feminine yelp. Staring down at her, I toy with her pussy, rubbing circles around her clit before running my fingers back up.

She's gorgeous, with her already slightly disheveled hair, and her lips parted in a perfect O.

"Already wet for me," I comment before unzipping my pants. The sound fills the room and the only other thing I can hear is her swallow.

Gripping the base of my cock, I pull myself out completely. Walking around to the front of my desk, I grip the hair at the nape of her neck, pull her back and position myself so she can suck. Which she doesn't do at first.

Instead she licks the bead of precum at my slit, and my toes curl before she wraps those gorgeous red lips around my cock.

She's careful about it, no doubt concerned her lipstick will be smeared.

If I wasn't in heaven from the pleasure she gives me, I'd smirk. That lipstick isn't going to last. As it is, she glides her tongue down my length and then takes me into her hot mouth.

My fist tightens as I watch her suck me down, her cheeks hollowing. Although I have a grip on her, she does it all herself, taking her time and tasting me.

"Enjoying yourself?" I question and then hold her in place, my cock firmly pressed against the back of her throat. She nearly sputters, swallowing me down even more. Her eyes glisten as she attempts to give an answering hum.

*Fucking gorgeous.*

"Good," I comment before thrusting deeper and then throat fucking her. Each stroke is deep and paired with a brutal pace. Her lips wrap around tighter and her hands come up but she's quick to put them back down.

When I pull out, her eyes watering as my signal, she takes in a heavy breath before I shove myself back in. With my left hand in her hair, I move my other to her throat and squeeze just slightly. Pushing my cock down deeper, I can feel my head in her throat and when she swallows, *fuck*, when she swallows—My spine tingles as my balls draw up and I have to stop myself.

I pull myself from her completely, satisfied from her heaving breaths and her mascara smudged around her eyes.

*Knock, knock.*

I've never felt such irrational anger. I'm the one who set this up and yet, it's fucking infuriating. Tucking myself back in, I'm quick to lay the skimpy dress over her backside, which doesn't cover much. "Don't you dare fucking move."

I wait for Braelynn to look at me before asking, "Did you hear me?" The deep flush in her cheeks deepens as she realizes we're about to have company. Her hesitant protest is quickly dissolved as I bend over her, kissing her shoulder and placing my hand on the back of her neck. I whisper, "I think you will enjoy this. Be a good girl for me."

With wide eyes and a short nod, she does what she's told. It's fucking addictive, the control she gives me. I crave more of it. All of it.

"Come in," I call out and Nate strides in.

"Boss—" His words falter, just as his steps when his gaze shifts from me to the gorgeous woman sprawled out on my desk.

With a head tilt, he waits.

"What is it?" I ask him as if there's nothing to be seen and take a seat.

# Braelynn

The air is cool against my bare skin. The desk is cooler. I still feel like I'm on fire.

The door opens with a creak, the footsteps sure and carrying an ease until they stop. Embarrassment, shame—I'm not sure what it is that heats my face but I know there's nothing I can do about it. Declan put me here how he wants me, and I don't dare stand up; hell, I don't know that I could move if I wanted to.

With my entire body paralyzed, and every nerve ending lit aflame from the forbidden aspect, I feel nothing but both wanted and ashamed.

Declan slides his hand beneath my dress as the two men take their seats. Declan is close enough to touch, while the other man, judging by the groan of the chair, is farther away and seated behind me, not in front.

The thin fabric of my dress barely covers part of my ass, and the rest of me is only hidden by the fact that I'm bent over. If I were to move, the dress would fall. My eyes beg to close, but I stare at the man who put me here. He radiates dominance but there's also a casualness to him. He has everything I don't have at this moment.

I'm only grateful that I can't see the other man. My eyes stay on Declan as he toys with me in a way that's almost relaxed despite another person in here watching. Declan's fingers slip up and down, moving from my swollen clit that begs for attention all the way up, pressing gently, testing me, then back down. Over and over.

"Should I come back later?" the man questions. I think I recognize his voice but I'm not sure. Part of me wonders if he knows who I am. I wonder what he thinks of me. Just as my mind begins to race, pleasure halts every burgeoning question in its tracks.

Declan pushes two fingers inside of me and slides them in and out, his rhythm slow, then moves back to my clit. My toes curl in my heels, the pleasure building and then sending a tingling need outward. My only movement is to grip the edge of the desk harder and squeeze my eyes shut tight.

I'm so close to the edge. I can feel it. It overwhelms me to the point that I can't focus on the conversation being held in the room. I can't focus on anything until Declan's hand slips away, leaving me wanting and he chuckles. It's deep and low and the man lets out a huff of a laugh but it's restrained.

As my high comes down, a sense of slight disappointment accompanies it. I stare at a beautifully paneled wall. There's not much to look at. There's everything to feel between my legs.

"I'm interrupting," the man comments. He has a deep

voice. Maybe he's one of the security men. Yes, I think that's where I recognize his voice from.

"No," says Declan. His tone is sharp enough to make me think the other man is right, that he's interrupting, but then Declan continues. "Go ahead."

"Some news from the city," the other man begins, and hesitates. "I've had a few different reports."

Declan hums and leans forward, forcing my gaze to his button-down shirt, until my eyelids fall shut once more with the divine pleasure from his touch. He toys with me again, rubbing ruthless circles against my clit until I let out a moan I wish I could stifle. If only I had something to bite down on.

"From our territories or others?"

"A couple from others." Their voices go back and forth, back and forth, but all I can feel is Declan. Declan's hand between my legs. He nudges my thighs apart a little further under the dress, and I know I'm not supposed to move other than this. He's good at what he does. And I fucking love it. I've wondered long enough and he's exceeded my expectations with a sinful flare I didn't know existed.

Flames are coming off my skin as arousal drips down the inside of one of my thighs. The intense sensation concentrates on my clit, building and building.

Hold still, I think and pray and desperately try to hold my position, but the other man is talking when it hits. The orgasm rips through me with a sudden shockwave. I close my lips tight and try not to make any sound. It comes out anyway. My heels lift off the floor. The movement makes the dress fall to the floor.

Fuck. Oh, fuck. There's not a shred of coverage. My heart pounds even as my climax tears through me.

Instantly, I know what I've done. I press myself flat against the desk.

Declan's hand is still between my legs. Slowly, he takes it out and puts it firmly on the small of my back. It's slick to the touch and my face heats all the more. "You disobeyed me."

"I'm sorry," I say in a breathy voice. It's a drunken concoction that takes over. I'd let him do anything he'd like to me. Hell, after what he's done, I'm barely capable of breathing.

He pauses. "Does that apology appear sincere to you?"

I realize after a beat that he's asking the other man in the room, not me.

"I would say, given the state she's in, it's a genuine apology."

Declan's hand presses down on my skin. "Thank Nate for sparing you of your first punishment, my little pet."

*Nate?* I don't know the other person in the room after all. Thank fuck for that.

"Thank you," I utter and it comes out just above a whisper.

"I think she'll be my good girl," he comments while lowering the tip of his nose to my shoulder. He leaves an openmouthed kiss there on my bare skin and a shudder of desire runs through me. "She'll learn to do better."

"I'm sure she will," our guest, Nate, comments.

By the time he's finished talking, I can feel Declan's breath on my neck, and on my cheek. His face comes close to mine. He kisses me and another shock moves through me. It's tender. Sweet. Soft. Nothing at all like he's been.

"Is she a new toy?" Nate asks.

Declan murmurs a hum in response.

The first sign that Nate's standing is the protest of the chair behind me. The next is the scrape of his shoe against the hardwood floor. I feel Nate get closer. His footsteps move in, and the air shifts. My heartbeat picks up again.

"Mind if I touch?" he questions, his voice above me. There's no doubt he could see all of me if only he dared to move two feet.

The possessiveness is unexpected in Declan's answer. As is the manner in which I revel in it. "Only if you want me to cut off your fucking hand. I don't share my toys." Declan opens a drawer in his desk, and a moment later I feel something soft between my legs. He cleans me up with the same gentle movements he used to kiss me. Who is this man? My mind can't take him in. Staying as still as I can, I swallow down my racing thoughts and watch Declan.

"Come," he says, but his hands show me what to do. Declan takes me into his lap and I settle into him, carefully covering myself and nestling into his lap. He wraps a black blanket around me and holds me close. With my eyes closed, I bury my head in the crook of his neck. His stubble is rough against my skin, but I take shelter in him.

Nate clears his throat. He says something about a man and train tracks. I can't pay attention to it. The softness of the blanket is too overwhelming, and underneath it is Declan's hard body. As he carries on the conversation, the deep rumble of his words vibrating through me, Declan runs his hand up and down my arm.

"Are you sure she's not undercover?" My eyes open wide in shock at that one, my body going stiff and I'm certain Declan notices it.

"She's not undercover," Declan tells Nate dismissively. "I've gone through her file. Just a pretty little pet." He looks down at me. "Aren't you?"

I lift my face to look into his eyes. "Like a cop? I'm not a cop." It makes me nervous to hear him even suggest it. But for once Declan's eyes are kind.

"Tell me what you are."

"What?"

"What exactly are you doing here and don't make me ask you again. What. Are. You. To. Me?"

"Your fuck toy, Declan." I barely breathe after saying the words.

"That's right. That's all you are, isn't it?" The kindness

in his eyes turns to desire. Nate coughs, and that same cold expression returns to his eyes. He's pissed. "Get out, Nate."

My body refuses to move a muscle as the man leaves. My gaze stays on Declan's although he doesn't look back. Not until the door has shut.

"You're hard to read tonight," he comments. "Do you like it when others watch?"

I don't know what to say to that. I came on his desk while another man was watching in the room.

"If you don't know," Declan continues, "that is an appropriate answer. Nate can be intimidating, and sometimes it's about who is watching." I shake my head. I don't know. I don't know if it was someone else in the room, or just Declan. Just the fact that he wanted me. "What did you hear of our conversation?"

"Nothing."

He toys with my bottom lip. "Did you miss the part where I told you all you are is my pretty little pet?"

"Don't—" Licking my lips, I hesitate but then summon the courage to speak. I bring up all the knowledge I have about arrangements like this between people. "Don't pets get a safe word?"

Declan chuckles and embarrassment lights my cheeks again. "A safe word," he repeats with a deadly grin. One that's both charming but condescending. "You'd like a safe word?"

I can only nod.

"What word?" he questions and I already know what word I'd use.

"Red."

His gaze searches mine and I have no idea what he's looking for. "I'll allow it. Another rule." His tone turns businesslike, although his arms remain cradling me. "You won't call me Declan in front of anyone ever again." His hand moves up to my knee, slides up to my thigh, and then he places it between my legs. As he cups my heat, I moan from the pressure he places on my clit. With my eyes closed he whispers at my neck, "Do I make myself clear?"

"Yes," I answer without hesitation. He rocks his palm, telling me what a good little pet I am for him. I'm already wet for him again. It's like he never stopped playing with me. "Here, it's fine. When it's us. But you will refer to me as Sir."

I nod, but then swallow nervously wondering if I should dare to voice my next condition. "I don't want to be called a toy or a pet to anyone else," I manage to say, though it makes me nervous to do it.

He pauses his movements and I peer up into his dark gaze. "Just between us?" he says. "You do like it, don't you?"

"I like it." My face reddens. It's true. I really do like it.

"Then what should I tell others you are, little pet of mine?"

"I don't know," I say on a breath.

"I could call you mine." My heart beats faster than it ever has, and harder. "You think you'd like that?"

"I think … I think I could manage to like it."

He makes a low noise and lifts me from his lap, spreading the blanket out on the desk and me along with it. One heel falls off and he doesn't give me a moment to retrieve it. I'm spread bare across his desk, wearing only my left heel. Declan's hands move fast at his belt and between my legs, and within moments he's pushing into me. Filling me and forcing a cry of pleasure from me. *Fuck.* "My little pet," he says as he thrusts into me with deep, long strokes. "Mine."

# CHAPTER 12

## BRAELYNN

Days go by in an exhausted haze.

I've never been this deliciously sore in my life. I'm sore from Declan.

It's a nine-to-five, so to speak; technically my workday starts at 6:00 at night and goes to nearly 3:00 in the morning. I do a lot of work with bookkeeping and records, but every moment I'm on edge and waiting. Being his personal pet, his toy, it's invigorating.

One moment I'm filing papers like he told me to, the next his hand wraps around the back of my neck and hours pass getting lost in his touch. Being used and fucked and then kissed like he needs to kiss me just to keep breathing.

Readjusting on the sofa, I'm hot and bothered all over

again. Even though I'm alone, I can't get the memories of the last few days out of my head, and I'm not sure I want to. His fingers between my legs. Nate's presence on the other side of the desk, watching. It's far dirtier than anything I imagined when Scarlet explained what the rooms on the lower floor were used for.

A smirk pulls up my lips and I hide it behind the throw blanket in my hand, pulling my knees up which elicits a slight pain from how sore I am.

I'm certain I know what's most addictive. It's like he can't get enough of me.

I'll think he's sated but then his eyes darken and I'm spread out on his desk again. Or bent over it. I take a sip of my chamomile tea and get comfortable with the blanket up over me. Rubbing my tired eyes, I note the day has come and gone and I spent most of it sleeping, unpacking here and there, but catching up on rest. With the dull drone of the TV serving as background noise, something's on the screen, but I couldn't tell you what.

It's not a real priority when Declan's on my mind. Nothing is a priority when I'm thinking about him.

I've never been fucked the way he fucks me. He's hard and possessive about it, and insatiable. I don't feel fragile with him. His intensity is like nothing I've ever encountered, and some parts of it do scare me, but at the same time ...

I think I'm falling for him a bit. For Declan Cross.

Nervous butterflies create a storm in the pit of my stomach and I combat it with a sip of tea. The man he grew up to be is nothing like that hollow-eyed boy in gym class. He has more secrets now, and he and his brothers have power. People fear them, and they should, because the Cross brothers aren't to be fucked with.

I know that. I'm all too aware of that truth. If nothing else, I love what we do together. I love what he does to me and how he makes me feel. I crave it. I want to be wanted by this man.

I was so afraid of that lower floor in The Club, but I've never felt better than when I'm in his office. My phone slides across the coffee table as it vibrates.

*Declan: Come in wearing the clothes I had delivered earlier.*

A flush warms my cheeks, even though no one is here to see me receive this text. The heat from my face follows a path between my legs. It's a good thing I was already sitting. What I feel about him is as intense as the way he looks at me. The lingerie he sent is the perfect example of his intensity.

Biting down on my lip, I think about the package that came today. The lingerie set I received is bloodred silk and lacy and must have cost a fortune. It came in a thick box, the kind that only comes from upscale boutiques with ladies behind the counter who never blush. It was probably handstitched somewhere.

This is what he wants me to wear, and he wants me to

wear it for him. It wasn't long ago that Declan commanded me to wear black at The Club, and to never wear red again. To wear it for now him feels that much more sinful.

He sent flowers yesterday along with my first check. It's ridiculous how much he's paying me. I nearly fainted at the sight of ten thousand dollars written out. The heaviness of the vase kept me upright.

It's easy to tell myself I may have made that had I continued to be a waitress and therefore I deserve the payment. But the truth of the matter is far more difficult to swallow.

It's also because all of these things, like gifts and money and lingerie. They almost make me feel like a whore. That's what whores do. They take money and gifts from men in exchange for sex. Growing up, I thought this was the one line I wouldn't cross. I might have terrible jobs and work in hot kitchens and put up with mean customers as a waitress, but I wouldn't sell my body to pay the bills.

Then you grow up. You realize sex is ... desirable. Not hooking up with strangers is more a matter of safety than anything else. And choosing the man you want. Then the emotions. It's messy and complicated, and oh my God. I groan, throwing my head back. With my hand over my face, I admit the truth.

I am Declan Cross's whore. Plain and simple.

That's a truth I'll never admit to my mother.

Now I understand what Scarlet was talking about before,

when she told me about the red dresses. When it's late, and the liquor is flowing, and these men look at you like they've never wanted anything more ... sometimes it's tempting. I get that now.

There is nothing more tempting than the way Declan looks at me when I open the door to his office. There's nothing more thrilling than getting a package delivered from him and opening it to find something beautiful and expensive. Men don't give you those kinds of gifts if they don't think they'll suit you. Declan thinks I'm worthy of these gifts, and not only that, he wants to see me in this gorgeous lingerie. He wants more than to know I received it, he wants to see the proof on my body. He wants to put his hands on it himself.

That's what Scarlet meant, but I feel it all the time, not just when it's late, and not just when the liquor is flowing. I feel like this all the time, even when I've had nothing to drink but chamomile tea.

It's different from taking random people down to the lower floor for a drunken fuck. That wouldn't be enough for Declan, just like sending me the lingerie isn't enough for him. It's not enough for me, either.

Stretching my tired body, I go back out to the kitchen and wash the cup from my tea in the sink, then settle it into a small rack to dry. I check the deadbolt on the door. Check my phone for any more messages and make sure it's plugged in. I give the curtains another tug to make sure no one can see inside. Although I've slept most of the day, I feel like I could sleep for a week right now.

Then I go back to my phone and return Declan's text.

*Braelynn: I will wear it, Sir.*

I have it all typed out and ready to send when something catches my attention from the TV. It was the word "Cross." The remote has fallen between the couch cushions but I dig it out and push down hard on the button to turn up the volume. Even with it louder, it's hard to make sense of what the news anchor is saying. Her voice is calm and even, and her gray blazer is so perfect that she can't possibly be talking about one of the Cross brothers, but she is.

She's also talking about a man named Marcus.

It hits me all over again that they're involved in things even the woman on the news won't say out loud. Dark things. Illegal things. The kind of things that make people put an extra deadbolt on the door at night. The Cross brothers have never shied away from the underbelly of the city, and now they're in charge of it.

Everyone knows it but no one can prove it. It takes me a moment to understand what she's saying. A number of cold cases are linked to both the mysterious grim reaper who used to terrorize the area, but now the crime family known as the Cross brothers are suspected.

The blood draining from my face chills every inch of me.

Fear makes my heart beat faster despite all the chamomile

and how tired I am. It's not just The Club I'm a part of now. The conversations I've overheard while with Declan ... I know the area the news anchor mentioned. I know the train tracks and I know Nate brought them up more than once.

Swallowing down the anxiousness, I close my eyes and my mind instantly goes back to the feeling of being wrapped up in that soft, black blanket he keeps stowed away in the bottom desk drawer to wrap me in when he's done with me.

He's strong underneath me, holding me tightly, kissing my hair.

I told him I heard nothing and I meant it. With the click of a button, the TV turns off.

All I know is that I am his and I haven't heard a damn thing.

Even that lie sends a deep chill to ice my veins. It's wrong. That's a real line I thought I'd never cross: turning a blind eye. I'm in over my head. I've been ignoring that, because it's easier. I don't want a confrontation with Declan. I don't want a confrontation at all.

But how am I supposed to do this? It's one thing to be a plaything and a pet. It's another thing if the man you belong to is a murderer.

Shivering, I glance at the black screen of the TV and then the stairs. If I had to, I could pack a bag right now and go. I could drive out of the city and keep driving until I saw an exit that looked appealing on the highway. Oh God, what would I do? Change my hair and try to get a job where people didn't see me often? Even if I did that, how long would it take for him to find me? I remember Nate's question, and thinking I could give Declan any reason to suspect I'm undercover or an informant sends true fear through me. I have no doubt Declan has influence beyond the city. I bet people would agree to whatever he said anywhere in the world. They can feel the power he has, and the dangerous energy.

Retreating to my bedroom, I take a seat on the bed. What I need is to know more about him. Scarlet would know more than I do. I bring up my texts and start to type one out, but it goes nowhere. Type. Delete. Type. Delete. I feel like I've been doing that a lot lately. But maybe I don't want these questions in a text.

Falling back, the cheap mattress bounces with me and I cover my face with both hands. I wish I hadn't seen the news.

Not out of fear or conflict. It's because I'm falling for him.

Already. I am so fucked.

# Chapter 13

## Declan

Her pussy is the prettiest shade of red after taking my cock. Swollen, used. Her right ass cheek is beautifully flushed from my grip while I took her.

She is the perfect distraction. I'm growing far too fond of this routine.

"Push it out," I whisper with a hand on each curve of her ass. Kneeling on my desk, her heels hang off the table and her cheek presses against the desktop along with her breasts. I started the day by getting her off sucking her clit, then I found my own release buried inside of her. Sleep didn't come easy last night. All I wanted to do was bury myself inside of her. I think her days off will need to come to an end. I'm far too greedy for that.

"I want to see my cum drip down that pretty little pussy," I tell her and she moans a sweet, strangled sound as her entrance clenches and my semen slowly leaks out of her slit and then drips down to her bare thigh.

My satisfaction is evident with a deep groan as I lean back into my chair.

"You could start a war, you know that?" I compliment her, my gaze shifting from her ass to her simper as she peeks over her shoulder toward me.

The blush she gives me is everything. As if she isn't completely aware of what she does to me.

It's been days of this. I thought I could fuck my interest in this out of her, but every day I want more. Testing her, playing with her, fucking her until I'm spent.

Nipple clamps lay heavy on my desk. Snapping them off during her climax left bright pink marks on either side of her breasts, and more importantly, had her screaming my name in pleasure. She came harder with those than she has anything else.

Even the vibrator didn't do it for her like the clamps did. Although, a bit of edging may have helped.

As I stand, opening the top drawer of my desk to put the clamps back, she moves. Lifting her upper body before I told her she could is going to get her in trouble.

Her obedience doesn't end once we've both come. She damn well knows that.

Tossing the clamps in without looking, I chastise her with the ease of being her Dominant.

"Did I tell you ..." I start and my hand raises to come down against her ass. I don't get to finish, though. The words are silenced as Braelynn cowers back. Notably, her arms raise as if I was going to strike her across her face.

*What the fuck?* Everything drops. It's like everything falls in that moment. That›s the only way to describe her split-second reaction.

Collapsing onto her back, she nearly falls off the desk and I have to brace her torso to keep that from happening. Hissing, I barely catch her. "The fuck are you doing?"

Tension pulls at every muscle as Braelynn stiffens. She swallows, and only then does she look up at me.

*What the hell just happened?*

"Braelynn." I say her name gentler before telling her to get back into position. My heart hammers in my chest.

Nodding she does so, eagerly, but fear is prominent in her gaze. My pulse doesn't stop pounding in my ears, though. She lays her head down with the other cheek resting against the desktop. Back to position like a good girl.

I take my time, zipping up my suit pants and buttoning my dress shirt after wiping her down and cleaning up the mess she made.

All the while she's silent, occasionally looking back at me, questions staring back at me.

Oh, my little pet, there are certainly questions coming.

Rolling up my sleeves, one by one, I stalk around the desk. "You thought I was going to hit you," I speak, focusing on my shirt.

She only moves to turn her head.

"I just ..." she trails off and swallows audibly.

"Yes. You did, didn't you?"

"Yes," she whispers.

There's a numbness that crawls over my skin. It's sick and cold, two things I've been dubbed more than a time or two.

I thought she was enjoying this. My mind travels back to the thought I chose to silence: *she could be doing this for ulterior motives.*

"Why would you think that?"

"I don't know," she murmurs, and refuses to look at me. I have to bend to grip her chin, my other hand bracing myself. Her wide, dark eyes peer back at me, begging me for something and I don't know what. "Is it because of that first night? When I hit that fucker who tried to sleep with you?" The cords in my neck tense. It was a fucking stupid thing to do. "I don't—"

"It's not you." She rushes out the words, cutting me off.

Letting go of her, she lies back the way she's meant to, and I take a guess. "Someone else hit you?"

She only nods and then sniffles like she may cry.

There's not a damn thing I like about any of this. Every

alarm is ringing, my body tense.

"Like this? Like I punish you by—"

"No. Not like this."

"Do you not enjoy this? Do you want to stop?"

Her words are rushed, "I don't know why I—" Tears brim at her eyes and I fucking hate it. "I don't know why I reacted like that."

"Are you going to cry?" I don't know what compels me to ask her. Of course she is. She's already crying.

My hand moves to the back of my head and I rake my hand up as she shakes her head as much as she can before saying, "I'm just embarrassed."

Her face reddens further as she attempts to hold back her tears.

Settling on what I have to do, my strides are purposeful as I wrap my arm around her waist. "Come here. You can get up. Come here."

With her small frame cradled in my arms, I move her to the chair. She does what she always does, clings to me, buries her head so I can't see her. And I do what I do, I hold her.

I prepare for her to cry, but she doesn't.

"Tell me what happened." I give her the command in a low murmur. Patience does not come easy. All the while we sit, I kiss her hair, and I stare ahead at the bookshelf, lined with a number of heavy trinkets I could so very easily bash against a man's skull.

"I was married. Young. At eighteen. I didn't know any better. We divorced."

Each statement is spoken quietly, carefully.

I already knew she'd been married, but I assumed it was done and over. It hadn't occurred to me that he'd tainted my little pet with reactions I can't control.

"And he hit you?" It's not so much a question as it is a statement.

Maneuvering in my lap, she sits up straighter, not a tear in sight. Her dark eyes search mine and I give her nothing. My expression is impassive.

She whispers, "A couple of times."

"His name?" I question, needing to make sure I'm certain of the man who put his hands on her in a way that left fear where all I crave is desire.

"Travis." With a short nod, I end the conversation.

Resting my nose against her hair, I take a moment breathing her in, staring ahead to calm myself. With even and steady breaths, I force my body to relax until my little pet rests easily against me once again, absolved of the heavy weight of her confession.

"Do you enjoy what we do?" I whisper the question and her answer is immediate. "I do."

It's a soothing balm, but only so much as it can cover.

When I kiss her temple, she relaxes further. I can't be sure she's already aware, so I tell her simply, "Any pain I give you will be heightened by pleasure tenfold and never out of anger, never to harm you."

My gaze is still straight ahead, her head nestled against my chest. She offers me a murmur of understanding, her warm breath tickling my throat.

Although it would seem as if the situation is settled, that statement can't be further from the truth.

My tone is firmer as I tell her, "I must punish you when you misbehave. Do I make myself clear?"

Her body stiffens slightly but she acknowledges what I've said quickly enough. "Yes."

"I didn't tell you to move and you did."

"I know," she answers, easier now, more accepting.

"I'll let you choose your punishment," I offer her in an attempt to assuage her worry.

"I'm sorry," she says as I help her up and onto her feet.

"Don't be sorry, I rather enjoy punishing you—" I begin to tell her, but she cuts me off.

"No. No," she says and glances up at me but she's quick to look away, biting her lower lip to silence herself. I don't miss how her fingers nervously intertwine around each other, or how she doesn't look at me in the least as I take her to the hidden door in the bookshelf. It opens with a single push.

# Chapter 14

## Braelynn

**H**oly fuck. Whips and all manner of implements for fucking hang in front of me. The door in the bookshelf hides so many toys and tools I don't know where to look first. The light shines off of metal handles and the muted black leather brings a scent of sin to engulf me.

There are at least a dozen whips. A fucking dozen. Some are longer, some have thinner strips of leather, and others aren't leather at all. I'd reach out and touch them, but it's all too shocking.

A shiver runs down my spine. Some of these are intimidating. More than intimidating—they honestly look like weapons intended to do severe damage.

"Do you like any of them?" Declan asks. His deep baritone

startles me and I take a step back, my hand over my chest.

I turn to face him, my heart in my throat. "Have you used all these before?"

He narrows his gaze, dropping down to my chest before answering. "They're new."

"No, like ... have you ..." I correct myself. "You know how to use them."

"Yes."

Tension remains between us. It's awkward, and not at all like it normally is. Or maybe it's just me. I don't know. I can't get out of my head. I genuinely thought he might hit me for a moment, not that *he* would. Not that *Declan* would ... but when I was lying down Travis used to hit me; he always waited until I was lying down. I can't shake the feeling. It was too much like the memory.

"Do you like any of them?" Declan questions again. Staring up at him, I wish I could tell him, but I don't want to go backward. Instead I focus on the collection of toys ... if you could even call them that.

I hug my arms to my chest and warm myself, running my hands up and down my exposed skin. It's a little cold. Or maybe it's my nerves. "Some of them scare me," I admit. There's a belt with studs hanging right at eye level. "This would hurt."

"Very much," Declan agrees, "but it wouldn't break your skin." Is he always so matter-of-fact like this? It feels different.

"You want to use it on me."

He nods. "I will use it on you, and you're going to fucking love it."

My heart races even faster. A lightheadedness takes over at the idea of having all these things used on me. I can trust him. I'm sure I can trust him. But something in my body isn't so sure. I just want to leave.

There's a knock at the door. Saving me, telling me I should go now. That I'm not in the right mindset for this. I can't shake the feeling of Travis's hands on me and I don't want to do this right now.

Fuck, I thought I was long over this. It takes everything in me not to cry. At the disappointment in myself, at the shame, at the fact that Travis did such a number on me.

I just want to be okay.

"One minute," Declan calls. Then his eyes are on mine again. "I have an appointment, so you'll have to wait. You haven't chosen your punishment, so this may count if you handle it well." His tone sounds hopeful. His lips even kick up into a smirk as he brushes my hair back. I could lean into that touch, his strength and his warmth, but he pulls away too quickly.

"You'll sit how I place you and stay just like that. It's called mental bondage."

Blinking, I question, "Mental?"

"Because the restraints are psychological." Declan leads

me back to his desk and guides me to the floor so I'm kneeling.

"I just ... stay like this?"

"Yes."

"For how long?"

"For as long as I'd like." The calm comes with this so-called punishment. Hell, I think I need it. Just a moment to sit and think. To get these thoughts out of my head rather than letting them stew.

Getting down on my knees, I peek up at him in all his authority. His hand runs down my hair as if he's petting me and I'm able to lean into it for just a moment. I shouldn't feel so comforted, but I do. It's Declan. Declan takes my hair in his fist, tilting my head and bends down to whisper in my ear. "You are mine, aren't you?"

It doesn't hurt, to be gripped and moved by him as if I'm a doll. "Yes," I whisper.

He pulls out a plush cushion and tells me to sit. It's black velvet and at least two by two feet. It's simple. Kneeling. Sitting. But I'm naked. He arranges my hands on my thighs and tips my chin up so I'm staring straight ahead. "Do not look at the floor," he orders.

"Yes, Sir."

My gaze shifts to my dress forming a puddle in front of his desk. He doesn't cover me, or make any move to grab my clothes as he calls out for whoever is at the door to come in. My face heats with embarrassment when the door opens and a man comes in. He sees me on the floor with a flick of his eyes.

I have no idea who he is.

Declan gestures to the desk like I'm not even there. "Have a seat."

"I like the furniture," the other man comments with a quiet laugh. Declan doesn't laugh. The look he gives the man is deadly.

The other man takes a seat across from Declan, and the conversation begins. Something about the docks and when a shipment is coming.

The news anchor comes to mind.

Every sordid rumor flicks through my mind. I can't stop it and when I do, I wish I hadn't.

It doesn't take long for my mind to fly back to when I was with Travis.

I wish I could stop thinking about him. Wish I could stop remembering everything he did. He used to embarrass me, purposefully. The memories are upsetting enough, and now I'm naked on a cushion. My skin heats, and my heart pounds. I swallow heavily. Declan and the man don't seem to notice my dilemma. Whoever he is, he keeps glancing over at me.

"What do you think?" Declan says, and it takes a moment for me to register that he's not speaking to me. Both of the men stare down at me expectantly.

"Is she in trouble?" he questions.

"A bit of a punishment, yes." The man readjusts in his seat

and nods with a grin. "She's doing very well if you ask me."

I hate that they talk about me in front of me. This is different from before. I nearly speak up, moving from this position until Declan's hand cups the back of my head and he says, "She's a good girl. Just had a moment earlier."

It's odd to feel such relief, such warmth, while also anger. A moment. It was just a moment for him. It's not one moment for me. My throat tightens, my emotions at war with one another.

The stranger asks, "Is she a new pet?"

"She's mine." Declan's tone is severe as he takes his hand away. I love his possessiveness, but it's not enough.

The conversation continues without me as the focus.

Travis comes to mind again, and it's too much. It's bringing up old emotions in a storm that won't go away. I feel trapped on this cushion, just as trapped as if he'd tied me up, and I can't stand it. It's like I can't breathe. I should have left. I don't want this. I can't do this. "I want out," I say, interrupting them.

Declan turns to look at me, his face blank. "If you want to come out, you'll need to tell me your punishment instead."

Anger crashes over me as tears prick the back of my eyes. "Fuck you."

"Get out," he says, so quickly it shocks me. But he's not telling me. He's speaking to the other man. The stranger's eyes go wide. "Get the fuck out."

# Chapter 15

## Declan

The door closes with a hurriedness in Joshua's steps and with barely restrained anger, I rise and make my way to her. She's no longer kneeling. Her arms are crossed over her chest as she sits on her ass, hiding herself from me. I command her, "Up now."

"I want to leave," she bites out, not bothering to even look at me.

"Like hell you're leaving before I redden your disrespectful ass," I grit out, my teeth clenched as I bend down to grab her. My entire being trembles with the need to punish her for speaking to me like that, then she doubles down, her words striking me with a force I couldn't predict.

"You're a psychopath."

It's as if she's slapped me. I'm far too careful as I rise, standing tall and commanding her, "Get up." I practically snarl. Why does she push me? Does she think I won't punish her? That I can't punish her in a way that won't trigger her like it did earlier. Or that I won't?

Heat bristles and I stay eerily still, waiting. "Stand up now, Braelynn." The sentence is spoken so softly she finally peeks up at me, her wide eyes reeling.

I don't know what the fuck happened. Something's gotten into her head. Did she think I'd go easy on her because another man hurt her? That she could push and I'd let her. Hell, does my little pet want a fight?

"Stand up now," I repeat and she finally obeys. "That's better."

"I just want to leave," she tells me and her voice trembles.

"Walk to the desk and get into position, now," I command her, ignoring her plea to leave. "Do not make this harder on yourself than you have to," I warn.

If she leaves now ... I don't think she'll ever come back. Chaos brews inside of me. *What the fuck happened?*

When she swallows, the cords in her neck tighten. Her arms are still loosely crossed in front of her. I watch as she takes the first step and then the next to the desk. She moves her clothes and then presses herself down, her legs spread, exactly how I like her.

*Good girl.*

The relief I feel is unexpected. Taking a step and then another, I watch her. The nervousness washes off of her in waves.

"Do you like pushing me?" I question.

"No," she answers immediately and her voice tightens. The hardened veneer of her expression crumbles in an instant. She's on the verge of tears again.

"Then what the fuck was that?"

"I don't know," she murmurs and her breath comes in a shudder. She turns her head, to look away from me.

"No. You will watch me and I will watch you," I order and with the harshness in my tone, she faces me. Something twists inside of me at the sight of her. Bent over, unraveling into utter vulnerability.

"That is my good little pet. Unravel for me."

Her shoulders heave as she attempts to calm herself.

"I'll pick your punishment for you." I move each hand where she can grip to keep her steady. "Don't move your hands off the edge of the desk."

Instantly I know exactly what instrument I'll use. The collection I curated for her can wait. The top drawer opens easily and a wooden ruler is lifted.

This will leave marks, welts perhaps.

"Every time you sit, you will think of how you chose to move from your kneel," I tell her before shutting the drawer and coming to position beside her.

I nearly put it back, but then I remember the "fuck you" and name-calling. I bring it down against her ass in a swift strike.

Her lips part, her upper body comes up, and she cries out in both shock and pain.

Her hands, though, they stay right where they should.

With the ruler hot in my right hand, my left splays against her shoulder blades, urging her back down.

Tears brim and then leak easily down her reddened face.

"You will keep count," I command.

"One," she whispers and then pulls her bottom lip into her mouth, taking the tears with it.

I'm quick to land the second an inch from the first, leaving a bright red stripe across her plush ass. Her back arches, and she holds back a cry. "Two."

I lower the next punishing blow to her upper thighs.

"Three," she utters, her knuckles turning white as she grips the edge.

Rubbing a soothing circle against the red marks makes her wince but when I squeeze, her mouth parts with a moan. She writhes for me.

That's what you do when you're in pain. You take hold of the wounds and turn them into sinful pleasure.

With that thought in mind, the next lashing lands between the first two. Spreading the marks, I take care not to strike the same place twice.

Another one lands and another. I move to stand behind her, fisting the ruler and lean over her draped form. When I press against her, only the fabric of my pants separating her from me, she protests with the most beautiful sound. Kissing down her neck, I grind myself against her and it morphs like it should, twisting that pain into the only thing I ever want her to feel.

"Just imagine how this is going to feel ..." I whisper down the curve of her neck before nipping her earlobe. Again she protests, pulling away as the sensations smother her. Grabbing her chin, I force her to look back at me to finish, "... when I fuck you like this and every thrust brings *this* with it."

My pulse races as I release her, those dark eyes swirling with every emotion imaginable. Her chest rises and falls just as mine does.

"Please stop," she begs just as my arm is raised, to color the other thigh with a stripe.

"You have three more, Braelynn." I pause, offering her mercy. I keep forgetting this is new to her. She said she wanted this, but does she even know what this relationship entails? "Or do you want to apologize?"

"I'm sorry I didn't stay still."

"For calling me a psychopath." The pain I felt leaks into the correction and I hate it. I hate all of this.

"You wouldn't let me leave," she says, turning slightly to face me. Whatever's written on my face, she sees it and her answering expression is one of sorrow.

"You didn't use your safe word. You never stopped it when you could have. You didn't even fucking try," I mutter with the disappointment evident.

She blinks, as if coming back to me from wherever the fuck she went. As if realizing the extent of what's occurred. "I'm sorry—"

"I would never call you a name to hurt you. I would never do *anything* to hurt you. Not real pain."

"I'm sorry. I'm sorry." She's quick to apologize and for a moment it seems like she'll turn to face me, to beg me, but her hands don't leave, they hold her back.

She has no idea how many times I've been called a psychopath by men who died minutes later. Their voices shriek at me from the depths of my memory. They were right. She's right. I'm a psychopath. I'm a murderer. I'm going to hell once I've finally been killed. I'll burn for the things I've done.

"Get your clothes on and get out."

I don't know where it's come from, but I need her to leave. With the emotion that swarms me, the realization of the power she has over me, to compel me to feel *this*, I can't be around her right now. "Now."

"Declan, I'm sorry," she repeats, slowly standing but not reaching for her clothes just yet.

"You can go home for the rest of the night," I add as I move away from her attempt to press her hands against my chest. Dropping the ruler to the drawer, I detach myself.

"Get dressed."

"Please, Declan. I'm sorry—"

"How many times must you make me repeat myself?"

"I'm sorry," she pleads as she obeys, slipping her dress over her head.

"... you would do anything to stay, wouldn't you?" I doubt if I should be so sure that she's not the one who's the informant.

"I didn't realize it would hurt you like that." Brushing her dark hair from her face, she tells me, standing awkwardly by the desk, "I don't want to hurt you."

"When you say that ... I believe you." A whisper at the back of my mind reminds me that this isn't some paid service or a rendezvous with a flame. She could be working with Scarlet. Using me. Fucking me just to get close. And yet, I can't stop the words from slipping out. "So don't hurt me. I don't ever want to hurt you either."

A shuddered breath shakes her shoulders as she nods up at me. "I won't hurt you. I promise," she tells me in lowly spoken words. Her longing gaze reflects an eagerness to start over, to leave all of this conflict behind.

Today has been difficult, between her admission regarding her abusive ex and our current dispute. There's a tension between us unlike what's been there before.

Glancing down at the desk, I consider telling her to

bite down on the ruler and fucking her from behind, giving both of us exactly what we need. That's all we need right now and then all of this goes away. It's what I'd planned on. Every thrust from behind would give her a hint of pain, heightening the pleasure. It's what she needs. I need it too. The haze that clouds my judgment vanishes as my phone rings, disrupting the moment.

It's Jase, no doubt with more information about the informants.

"Declan?" My name is a whispered and cautious question on her lips. Her cheeks are blotchy and her hair disheveled. I should love this look on her, this obvious need to make things right with me, but I loathe it.

*What the fuck am I even doing with her?*

"Get your shoes on," I command her and she's quick to move. I assume in hopes that this conversation is over, but it is far from over. "If you behave like that again, I'll lock you in a real cage." Pausing in her movements, she peers back at me silently. "Do you understand?"

She nods and swallows thickly before saying, "Yes."

The phone rings once more and I answer it. "One second." Bringing the phone down to my chest, I watch as Braelynn fixes the sleeve of her sweater dress. It's not until she's somewhat composed that I speak.

Although it's more than evident that she's emotional and still shaken.

"If you keep secrets from me, I won't know and you're going to end up hurting yourself." Fully clothed, she stares back at me with her eyes glistening, her arms crossed over her chest. Her bottom lip wobbles and the thoughts that flit through my mind are insane. Truly deranged.

The desire to hang up on my brother, to coddle her and love on her until she doesn't look at me like that any longer ... it's unfathomable.

So I do what's best for her, what I should have done from the very beginning. "Go home, Braelynn." She should have left the first time I warned her and never come back.

She doesn't respond verbally, only with a single nod before briskly leaving.

The moment the door closes and I answer my brother, all I can think is she might do just that after today.

She may never come back. It leaves me with a sinking feeling in my chest, and a chill and numbness that stay with me for the remainder of the night and into early morning. I stay up the entire time knowing all too well, if she were smart, she'd never step foot in this office again.

# Chapter 16

## Braelynn

Last night I cried over Declan Cross.

I don't know that I can do this. It's not just money and lust. I'm not okay and I keep crying every time I glance at the clock. With the shift of the red digital display, it turns to 4:00. I have two hours before I'm supposed to go back to him and my stomach is still in knots.

Rubbing my eyes, I splash cold water against my face and rub them again.

I'm so torn on what to do, I feel both drained and sick.

It's been two weeks since I started working for him, but it feels like a lifetime. I swear a part of me feels as if I know him, but he doesn't know me and really, what do I know about him?

Other than this compulsive need to be beside him. The

only thing I've done today is stare at the expensive bottle of wine he had delivered this morning. My check came wrapped around it. Does he think that will make this better? More importantly, am I supposed to pretend yesterday didn't happen? Am I supposed to be okay with this?

I collapse onto the sofa, peeking at the clock again and wishing I could pause time. Just enough to feel better, even a hint better. As every minute ticks by, it all feels heavier.

I'm still on the couch, wrapped in my blanket, when I get a text from Amy. She's a friend from a lifetime ago, and the perfect kind to have. She checks up on me here and there since moving to California to start a better life, but there's never any pressure between us. We always pick up right where we left off. It's good, because sometimes my life goes through drastic changes. Like when I left Travis. It never shocked her; she only wanted to make sure I was okay. She was the first person I told when he hit me. We were young and dumb and only nineteen.

I'll never forget that lonely feeling, like I couldn't tell anyone. I could always tell Amy everything, though. And she could do the same for me.

*Amy: How's the new job going?*

Honesty is not at the tip of my tongue. I tap out a text telling her it's all fine, just getting up to speed still, and send it. Chewing the inside of my cheek, it feels like I'm back years ago. Hiding from the truth and unwilling to tell a soul. When deep inside I want to scream it.

Maybe I should show up drunk, thank him for the bottle that sits on the coffee table, and then quit. That's what a very large piece of me wants to do.

Just as the thought crosses my mind, there's a knock on the door. I abandon my blanket and pad over. I check the peephole first.

Fuck. My blood goes cold and a nervousness rattles through me.

"Braelynn." His voice is calm as he looks directly at the peephole. "Open the door."

At the sight of Declan standing outside the door, goosebumps cover my skin. I fumble for the knob and pull it open.

His strides are steady and firm. His frame is so large in the small foyer.

He walks in with no hesitation, as if he owns this place as much as he owns The Club. It's so shocking to see him here, especially given last night, that I don't notice the bags at first. He holds up takeout. Chinese food, from the scent. It only takes him one look around to find the kitchen. His worn jeans and gray Henley are a change from the norm. As is all of this.

By the time I've shut the door, he's going through the cupboards and pulling out plates. He rummages through the drawers until he finds the forks and knives, then pulls paper napkins from a holder on the countertop and wraps two sets of utensils.

My arms crossed over my thin sleep shirt, I dare to ask, "What are you doing?" Tucking my hair behind my ears, I remember I look like hell. Not an ounce of makeup and my hair is a frizzy mess.

"Feeding you," he says, matter-of-factly. I watch him put food on the plates, his hands capable on the boxes. He glances to his right, to what should be a dining room but the table itself is still absent. Then he glances to the left, the living room, which is small and still filled with boxes. "Where do you like to eat?" he asks casually.

I take a moment, watching him. There's something different, calmer and more relaxed, but he also doesn't look me in the eye.

"The couch, mostly," I admit. "It's not the classiest thing in the world, I guess, but I like to flip through the channels while I eat."

He nods, "'Cause you're alone ..." he peers back at me, "when you eat."

There's a touch of sadness in his tone that catches me off guard. "Yeah."

He nods and then carries both of the plates and silverware out to the living room, setting it all on the coffee table.

As I take the seat beside him on the sofa, the couch groans. It's so cheap beneath him. My face feels hot with him seeing this part of my life, even though there's nothing special about sitting on my own couch. He takes the seat next to me.

"You didn't have to do this," I whisper. I'm starving and my stomach growls in protest of my statement. I could devour this plate in an instant. Instead the fork teeters in my hand.

"Yes I did." His answer is immediate.

"You could have called," I suggest, staring at his profile and willing him to look back at me.

"I was afraid you would tell me," he starts, taking in a deep breath, and staring ahead before he falls silent. A car honks its horn outside, sounding like it's coming from the parking lot of the yoga studio across the street.

"I can be ... a lot," he says, after a minute. The sound of him swallowing is the loudest thing in the room. "It's been a while and I forget sometimes ..." He seems to consider his next words. "I need you to communicate with me very openly. Very, very openly."

"What do you mean?" My ears burn.

"If I ask you what happened or why you feel a certain way, I need you to be blunt." He licks his bottom lip and then stares deep into my eyes. "I'm not good at guessing, Braelynn. And I don't want to hurt you. I want you to tell me everything."

The way he stares at me, as if he needs this, he needs me as if he's begging me, I can hardly sit so close to him. The air in the room seems to thin and it's only the two of us.

Neither of us eats, neither of us moves.

"I need you to forgive me and help me so I can handle you better."

"You're sorry?"

His jaw clenches at my question and I think for a moment I shouldn't have said it. "I can't fucking stand what happened yesterday and I keep thinking where I went wrong. I will not let a meeting interrupt us again. Never. Until I'm satisfied that you are well, no one will distract me."

Emotions create a storm around me as he tells me, "I want you to walk me through everything that happened so I can understand. I need you to, Braelynn. I have to know where I went wrong and I think I know, but I need to be sure because what happened ... it cannot happen again."

"What if I don't want to talk about it?" I question in a whisper.

His fork hits the coffee table with frustration.

"I am not a good man. Every rumor, every whisper you've ever heard ... consider them to be true. Even the most fucked up. Even the most depraved. It's all true. Knowing that, do you think I have the capacity for mercy?" The cords in his neck tense and tighten as he stares at me with a longing in his dark eyes.

"Do you think that if you don't tell me, that I will know limits and boundaries?" His voice is tight as he whispers the question, "Do you think I'll know when I hurt you?" My gaze slips from his lips, back up to his tortured eyes. "Because if you think I'll know, you should run. You should run far away. If you don't tell me, I will destroy you without even realizing it."

Of all the things to question, all I want to know is, "Will you tell me everything too?"

"It depends on what you ask."

My mind races with every question that's bubbled to the surface since that first day I saw him in his office. Before I can ask a single one, Declan starts.

"Your ex hit you. And it triggered you to see me over you?"

I nod.

"Does it matter what side?"

"What?"

"When he hit you, did he always come to a certain side? Is that what did it? I need to know what triggered it, because I quite like spanking your ass when you disobey me. Do you?"

My face heats and my thumbs play with one another. "Yes. I like it when you do that." Just talking about it brings back the lust for him and what we do.

"So ... do you know if there's something I did?"

The memories flit by and I know in an instant. "It was when I'd lie down, he'd wait and come up to the bed on my right side."

"Do you think that's it?" he questions after nodding.

I almost tell him I don't know again. Instead I offer, "If I think of anything, I'll tell you."

He hums in appreciation. "Good girl. Now, do you like it

when I call you my pet and fuck toy?"

"Yes." My answer comes with an eagerness and I slip my hand over his. His thumb rubs soothing circles and his gaze drops for a moment to where we touch.

Rather than waiting for me to push further, he questions, "Yesterday ... you didn't like being naked in front of Joshua? Or you didn't like the position. You didn't like what, exactly? What was it that made you want to leave?"

I swallow thickly, remembering the embarrassment. "I didn't like being naked in front of him ... like that."

"It will never happen again."

"I know I was before but—"

"You do not have to explain yourself. You don't want to be naked in front of other men. Fine. I love your body, I love that you're mine, but showing you off isn't something I need. It won't happen again."

Blinking, I let each and every statement sink in. He loves that I'm his. He said *love*.

"What else? There was something before that. I know there was." He waits, hunched over the plate, the fork tapping against the table. He stares back at me expectantly.

"Sometimes I go to a dark place and I have a problem getting out of it."

"What took you there?"

"I don't know," I answer honestly. He turns away for a moment, clearly frustrated and I don't want to lose him so I offer what I know to be true and tell him, "I just wanted you to hold me." My answer is tight as tears brim. I drop the fork and cover my face before I can cry, hiding from him.

He doesn't let me, though, he pulls me into his lap in an instant.

"I can do that," he whispers into my hair and it tickles down my neck and shoulders. He shushes me, rubs soothing circles down my back and it keeps the sobs away. It only takes a moment of him rocking me, holding me close, of breathing him in, to calm whatever it was that wrecked my composure.

After a moment I pull away. My hands press against his chest, just to put distance there. I part my lips to thank him or apologize or something, but he stops it all, every word, every thought with the way he looks down at me.

"If you need me to hold you, tell me. I can do that. I like holding you."

Nodding, I climb out of his lap and retake my spot. It's so overwhelming my hands tremble when I grab the fork.

"Is everything okay?" I ask him, feeling a vulnerability that threatens to dismantle me.

He nods and then clears his throat. "I think so. So long as you still want to be mine."

Nodding, I tell him I do. It feels like I'm on the cusp of falling. Part of me instinctually craves whatever Declan will give me, while the other part wants to run because it's obvious there's no going back from this.

"Can we eat?" I suggest in a murmur, pushing the rice around with my fork.

"I need to know if that's it, Braelynn."

"I think that's it."

"Are you all right?" Nodding, I do what I can to stay upright and just breathe. "You're intense, Declan."

"I've been called worse."

It's silent for a long moment while we pick away at the food slowly, and I can hardly stand it. All the while I want to kiss him, to touch him. But I don't.

"You have questions for me?" he asks, having barely eaten and sitting back on the sofa.

I swallow a bite of fried rice. "When was the last time you had a girlfriend?"

He huffs a laugh that breaks the tension and I peek over at him, his smile soothing something inside of me. A simper pulls at my lips.

"Never." He watches me lift the fork to my lips again. "Is that what you think this is?"

I don't know how to respond. I don't know what to think of us at all. Maybe we're just two broken pieces trying to fit together, but cutting each other instead.

"I think what this is and what we are ... requires me to open that bottle of wine," I suggest, taking a deep, steadying breath.

"I think we need something ..." Declan agrees, his gaze roaming down my body. There's an immediate warmth from the hungry look he gives me. His shoulders straighten when he tells me, "Take your clothes off, I don't want to ruin them."

Standing abruptly, he leaves me sitting there, speechless and paralyzed as he takes long strides to the kitchen. "Don't make me repeat myself," he warns and I'm quick to strip my sleep shirt off.

I can hear him rattling around, and he reappears a minute later with the bottle of wine in his hand. "What I want," he stresses as he sets the bottle down and then clears off the coffee table, "is to get drunk off of you."

"Lie down," he commands and I do as he says without thinking twice. In a swift move, he takes his shirt off over his head. The sight of his rippled muscles, the evidence of his powerful body, brings out a primal need.

I'm naked, trembling, wanting him and Declan comes to stand over me. He opens the bottle of wine, his eyes flashing. "Open your mouth, like a good little pet."

A shiver of desire comes over me as his hand rests on the dip in my hip, so close to where I need him.

I obey, and he tips the bottle over my lips. Wine flows directly into my mouth, but he doesn't let me drink much of it. He moves the bottle over my body, letting wine splash on my skin, and I shiver from the contact. Declan's on his knees a second later. His hand slips between my thighs as he licks up the bit of wine.

His tongue is rough and hot on my flesh, moving over

sensitive areas, licking and licking until he's had all the wine. My nipples harden and a wave of desire rushes to my most sensitive bits. My hand flies to his hair, and he tsks.

"Now, now, be a good girl. You know better," he gentles his tone with these words and I nod, placing a hand on each edge of the coffee table.

He runs his nose down my navel and then lower before kissing just above my clit, teasing me and forcing me to protest in a small moan. He chuckles, deep and masculine, the warmth of it keeping me on edge.

In between openmouthed kisses, he pours more wine that pools in my navel, sucking it up and then giving me more. He toys with my body, swirling his tongue over my nipples, nipping and biting. More often than not, I'm given the wine and he devours my body without it until his hands are on my inner thighs, parting my legs. He groans against my clit before licking and sucking it into his mouth.

I'm on the verge of coming already by the time he kneels between my legs and puts his mouth there. His tongue works me over. I'm instantly on the edge as he toys with me, nibbling and licking while he holds my thighs apart. The pleasure builds and my back arches. He keeps me down, his grip nearly bruising.

I let myself fall into it, feeling the weight of the last twenty-four hours melt away into nothing. I cry out his name as I come on his tongue and he murmurs, "That's it, little pet."

Exhaustion weighs down on me after I find my release. I'm tired from the long day without him and tired from the orgasm. Without much sleep, and with the bit of wine, I could sleep here on this coffee table, I could drift away right here, right now.

That's how damn tired I am. I'm pulled into Declan's arms and my arms wrap around his neck, holding myself as close to him as I can be. He carries me to the sofa and drapes the blanket around me, kissing my temple. His thumb tilts my chin up and his lips meet mine; at first they're gentle, but he deepens our kiss. He takes from me in that kiss and I moan from its intensity.

When he breaks it, I'm reminded of something I confessed long ago to Amy: All I want is a man who's going to fuck me and then hold me afterward. That's exactly what Declan's doing. I close my eyes and try not to think about it.

But I can feel him watching, so I open my eyes again. "What?"

"Nothing," he whispers and then rests his head on the back of the sofa. He shifts the way he's sitting so he can rub at his shoulder.

"Are you sore?" I wriggle up from his lap, and when I'm standing he raises his eyebrows at me. "I used to do massage. Let me."

Declan gives me a suspicious look, but he turns over on the sofa and stretches out. With him laid out, I realize just how broad his shoulders are. Just how powerfully his body is built.

Warming my hands, I wish I had oil so I could do a better job. He's so tight, the muscles barely loosen up. I get to work on his shoulders first. Deep, hard strokes for a deep tissue massage.

I'm rewarded with a groan I could easily become addicted to.

"Does that feel good?" I ask him, watching his eyes close. He hums a response.

Kneading his muscles, I realize just how tense he is. "Tell me if it hurts," I murmur, but I'm not sure he hears me. He groans, and then again a minute later.

"You were a masseuse?" he questions, his tone sleepy as I work his back.

"Yeah, for a year or so ... a while ago."

"Why did you stop?" he asks and lets out another groan.

"Travis didn't want me touching other men." My lips turn down at the memory. "He made a scene at the spa I worked at."

"Your ex sounds like a problem."

"He used to be." I speak without thinking, focusing on his shoulder. "You're really tight here." I'm hesitant, not wanting to hurt him, but there's a knot that won't give.

"Don't stop."

I put my hands back on his body. Declan's melting into the couch. "I pulled it a while ago," he says. "Tore a ligament."

"How did you do that?"

"When I was like, seventeen I think, my brother and I were running from ... I don't know," he tells me with his eyes closed. "Maybe ten or a dozen guys. So, very outnumbered."

"Running from them?" I keep up the strokes, running along the lines of his muscles as they relax under my touch. "It was a deal gone wrong. They set us up."

My hands pause as I realize what he's telling me.

"They had their guns pulled but we took off, ran behind this row of buildings." He swallows and as I press down along his back, stretching the muscles, his expression is so serene with his eyes closed, even if the story he tells me chills me to the bone. "There was an alley and behind it a fence. My brothers jumped first and then I was right there, but my shirt caught."

He pulls his arm behind him, letting his finger trail down a faint scar. "I got scraped up from it pretty bad, but I was stuck. Separated my shoulder."

Adrenaline courses through me at the thought of what he's describing.

"You were just hanging there? With your brothers ahead and the other men behind you?" I'm grateful his eyes are still closed, because my expression must show the terror I feel for him.

"No, they didn't go ahead. I screamed when it happened."

"So?" I feel the blood drain from my face.

"We had guns too. We made it out, Jase got hit in the shoulder, I had my fucked-up shoulder. Carter and Daniel went around the house for weeks making fun of it, pretending to injure their shoulders so they could fit in." A faint smile grows on his face at the memory.

I'm careful in between strokes to keep my breathing even so I don't let on.

Seventeen years old and he was in a shoot-out. He could have died. That's when I realize, he killed someone at seventeen. When I knew him. He had already committed murder.

We were only kids.

Questions pile up and I swallow them all down. I hurt for him. I hurt for all of them as the silence settles comfortably around us.

The thing about pain like that is it never seems to go away. "I'm sorry," I whisper.

He doesn't answer.

I keep massaging his shoulder, easing up on the pressure. When I peek down at him ... his eyes are closed. His breathing is deep and even.

Declan fell asleep on my couch. Sound asleep.

I let my hands go still. He looks so peaceful. I can't possibly wake him. I can't lie here with him either, because he takes up the full width of the sofa.

What am I supposed to do now that he's asleep? I find

myself going to get him a pillow and a blanket before I can overthink it. His story dwells in the back of my mind. His confession earlier about every rumor being true. There's a darkness to Declan that's very real. It's all I can think as I make my way upstairs.

In the bedroom, I open the closet door and tug the pillow down. I've got a box on top of it, so I do it gently. I don't want a big thud to startle him awake. I have the box out of the way and I'm getting the blanket when his voice comes from the doorway.

"Did you drug me?"

Fuck! I can't stop myself from gasping, my hand flying to my throat. "Declan. You scared the shit out of me."

His eyes are dark and suspicious, bordering on angry as he stands a good ten feet away in the doorframe of my bedroom. "Answer me."

"No." My heart is going to jump out of my body. "Of course not." He stares at me, looking in my eyes like he doesn't believe me. "You fell asleep. I was getting these for you." I hold up the pillow and the blanket to show him. It's insane he thinks that and I almost say it. But then I remember calling him a psychopath and I bite my tongue.

It's more than evident that he's paranoid, but I would never do that.

"I would never," I tell him, stressing each word. "You fell asleep and I was just getting you these so you'd be comfortable.

I didn't want to wake you up."

He doesn't say anything for a long moment.

Although my heart calms slightly, everything is on edge. "I didn't drug you, Declan."

He nods, although his eyes search mine and then he glances around the room as if he's looking for something before running a hand over his face.

In the back of my head a voice screams, *Say something*, and I don't know if it's yelling at me or if the command is meant for him. Another moment passes in silence and the passage of time creates more space between us.

"I'm going home. Good night, Braelynn." Remorse coats his farewell.

"Wait," I call out in a breath, dropping the pillow and blanket. "Don't go."

"I have to."

"Please, kiss me first." I bite my tongue before the explanation can get out. I don't feel right. It feels off again. I don't want us to go back to the tension that was there. "Just kiss me good night?"

A beat passes my uncertain heart before he stalks toward me, both of his hands around my face and he kisses me with a possessiveness and a need that stuns me. His lips press against mine, his tongue parts the seam and he devours me, brutally taking until my back is pressed against the wall.

When he breaks the kiss, I have to catch my breath.

"Good night, Braelynn."

Declan turns on his heel, and I can hear him leaving the house. I move to follow but the door closes. A car starts up outside, and by the time I reach the door, it's gone.

Declan Cross is a brutal storm, unforgiving and reckless. That's all I can think as I sit on the stoop, wishing I had the pillow still so I could hold on to something.

To anything other than the dark tales of a man who never had a chance to live a life other than this hell he was born into.

# Chapter 17

## Declan

I haven't been able to sleep easily for as long as I can remember.

Sleep evades me. Day in and day out, exhaustion wears me down and begs for me to rest. Yet when I lay, my mind keeps me up, replaying every moment of my life that led to where my family is now. I can admit that two years of taking on this business relatively on my own has made me paranoid. I've been screwed over by more people than I can trust. In fact, the only person other than my brothers who I trust implicitly is Seth. And I barely see any of them anymore.

So staring down at the results from the blood work, I don't believe it.

Braelynn didn't drug me. I simply fell asleep, in a strange

place, without any protection whatsoever.

It's as reckless as it is unbelievable.

*Knock, knock, knock.*

It's a bit too early to be Braelynn, although perhaps she's as eager to see me as I am her. Checking the cameras, I'm surprised by my disappointment that she didn't come in early.

"Come in," I call out as I click out of the results the doctor sent me, and over to the profile for Travis Marks.

The gray profile photo of a man with a smirk stares back at me. He's a man who needs to die. What happened is his fault, I'm certain of it. His existence is problematic.

"Boss." Nate greets me at the same time that Jase says, "We need to talk."

The two of them beside one another is an intimidating sight. Nate's scar on his chin adds to his severe and rugged countenance. My brother is taller but only by an inch or two, and Nate's bulk more than makes up for it.

Marcus sent him to me two years ago as a part of our deal. His men. My rules. ... so that he could escape. He didn't tell me why he had to leave, only that something broken long ago needed to be fixed.

"You're slipping," Jase comments, a smirk on his lips as he drags the corner chair closer to my desk and Nate takes a seat.

A crease settles between my eyes. "How so?"

"Your door was unlocked last night. I walked right in and you weren't here." Jase appears proud of himself, but my dead stare has him thinking better of it.

"There's no way in hell I left without locking it."

My brother narrows his eyes, the severity of my response catching him off guard.

Nate's cough interrupts the tension.

"That's ... it's fine. It's not why we came."

My shoulders tense and I glance back to the computer, to the black and white photo of a man I wish was here so I could release this pressure building inside of me. Cracking my knuckles, I lean back in the chair and ask, "What's going on?"

"You all right?" Jase asks as Nate states, "Someone else is with them."

I glance at my brother, his expression questioning before focusing on Nate.

"Another informant?" Heat tingles at the back of my neck.

"No, someone ... someone who also wants information."

"What do you mean?"

Jase answers this time, "The cops are sending someone else information. Not us and not the feds." He crosses an ankle over his knee. "Someone is lining their pockets and it isn't us."

Nate nods.

*Fuck.* The list of enemies grows every fucking day.

"We have a meeting with Carter tomorrow to work out the possibilities. Anyone who seems off."

"We need the footage," Nate requests.

"I've already gone through the tapes of every man who's been with Scarlet in the past two years."

"And?"

"She has her preferences but they're all still cooperative."

Jase seems to consider what it could mean. Is she meeting with men who she wants information on, or is one of them the man she's giving the information to?

There are too many questions and not enough answers.

Nodding, I tell them, "I'll bring the list tomorrow."

Jase's hands tap down in unison on the armrests. "All right then."

Both Nate and he stand, adjusting their ties and buttoning their navy and dark gray suit jackets, respectively. Where Nate couldn't possibly pass as a gentleman or someone born into wealth, Jase could fool the world with his charming smile. I wasn't gifted with that perceived glamour. Slipping his hands into his pockets, Jase questions again, more casually although it's anything but. He can't hide the concern in his eyes. "Everything else okay?"

"Fine," I answer.

"Where were you last night?" He shifts uncomfortably.

"Worried about me?" I smirk at him with my joking response.

His downturned expression makes me regret it. "I'm still your big brother." As he cracks a grin, Nate and I chuckle. "You should come home for dinner Saturday ... or Sunday."

"I'm sure I can make it."

"Good." Jase gives an easy smile as he turns to leave and I reciprocate it.

"Hey Nate, stay for a moment." Jase looks between us and gestures a goodbye before leaving. When the door's closed, I ask Nate, "What happened to Braelynn's ex-husband?"

"I'm not sure, Boss … What happened to him?"

"I believe he got intoxicated and tripped on the train tracks."

"That sounds tragic," he comments. And the dark look we share speaks volumes.

"It is." I murmur, "Such a senseless way to die."

"And when did that happen?" He gives me an expectant look.

"I would have liked tonight, but let's stick with his habits. He often goes out Thursday evenings."

"Understood." With his response, I exit out of the photo, and rid myself of the problem once and for all.

"Is that all, Boss?"

"Yes. Thank you, Nate."

Just as he prepares to leave, there's a knock at the office door.

Checking the cameras, my pulse races and a heat gathers along my skin. A different heat, the kind I crave. My little pet is early after all.

"When you leave, keep the door open for her, will you?"

Nate's smile is knowing. "Of course."

I don't miss Braelynn's wide eyes of surprise as Nate

opens the door. "Braelynn," he greets her and she flushes. "Have a good night." He keeps his distance, professional but friendly. His gaze moves to mine with an easy nod before the door closes, leaving her alone with me.

Her movements are nervous as she tucks a stray lock of dark brown hair behind her ear.

"You look beautiful tonight," I tell her, my voice softer and deeper than anticipated. Coated in the sinful thoughts that filter into my mind.

Of me fisting her perfectly curled hair, of me smearing that lipstick with a brutal kiss. Of me ripping that loose lace blouse off of her, lifting her skirt up and fucking her against the wall. We haven't made use of most of the surfaces in here. I aim to change that as quickly as possible. I want memories of her everywhere I look.

"Thank you," she whispers and questions, "should I—"

"I know I left in a bit of a rush last night," I interrupt her and push my chair out, patting my lap. "Come here."

She's quick to come to me, removing her heels to settle down in my lap. Her deep brown eyes never leave mine like they're searching for something.

With both hands braced on my shoulders, she faces me with an expectantly look. My right hand settles on her hip, my left brushes her hair back from her face and I stare down at those bloodred lips of hers.

"I have problems sleeping, so when I woke up it was …"

I lift my gaze to hers to complete the thought, "... alarming."

"I'm sorry," she whispers.

"You're apologizing because I fell asleep and then scared the shit out of you?" I shake my head at her. She's sweet and innocent. She has compassion and empathy where I do not. The last thing I want to do is tarnish it. I want to keep her like this for as long as I can.

"I'm sorry you were alarmed."

"It's not your fault. I think you know by now, I have issues. I'm not a good man, but I'll do what I can to be good to you."

My admission rewards me with a shy flush from my good, sweet girl.

"You're better now?"

Leaning back, I move my hand under her, readjusting and pulling my cock out.

"I will be shortly."

As she tries to maneuver herself to remove her undergarment, I reach up, smirking when I feel the lace. My thumb easily pushes through them, shredding them and rewarding me with a gasp from my sweet girl.

Leaning forward, I silence it with a kiss, stealing the air from her and massaging her tongue with mine. With my hands up her skirt, my fingers move to her hot center and toy with her, rubbing her clit, slipping my fingers through her slit and then back up until she moans in my mouth.

Her fingers dig into my shoulders and I revel in how greedy her touch is.

With my lips still against hers, I murmur, "Already wet for me."

"I want you," she whispers back with a sincerity and need I didn't realize I was desperate for.

In one swift move I position her how I need and impale her on my cock.

She falls forward, moaning my name and clinging to me as I wrap one hand around her shoulder, my arm bracing her back and holding her steady while I fuck her.

Her moans are drawn out and her warm breath travels down my back as she bites down on the curve of my neck in an attempt to silence herself.

A cold sweat breaks out along my skin and I relish in it. Nothing else matters as I murmur into her ear that I need her more than I need anything or anyone.

Her nails dig into my skin as she holds on. She's close. I know she is as she tightens around my cock, writhing in my arms.

As she calls out my name, her neck arching and her release taking over, I devour her lips with mine and that's what does it. Capturing her kiss, I come undone with her.

# Chapter 18

## Braelynn

The mall is busy and humming with people as Scarlet and I stroll through the wide, tiled hallway. I've always loved the mall. The crowds, the food court, the shops and sales. It's full of life. This particular mall is one of my favorites. It has high ceilings and a second floor with endless stores to shop and get lost in.

"We're here," Scarlet says with a grin. "Are you sure you're ready for this?"

I take another sip of my latte and smile back at her over the cup. "Hell yes I am."

We enter an excessively large home goods store, one of my favorite places to shop, and both of us grab carts from a row near the door. We wander through each aisle, picking up items and putting them back down. More than a few go into my cart. A new set of dish towels. A pretty shower curtain. It's freeing to be able to put my own touches on my place. I can decorate however I want and it wasn't until this moment that the realization hits me. I've never had a place of my own. I've never truly been on my own.

"What do you think of this?" I ask Scarlet, holding up a welcome mat.

"Oh my God, 'Take off your shoes and bring in the booze?' It's cute," she says. "It's so you. Get it."

I toss it into the cart with a smile that won't quit. It comes with another new feeling too. Declan pays me so well that I don't have to calculate the cost down to the penny and hunt for a coupon. I still have a coupon, though. I wouldn't come to this store without one.

I might be saving up, but I would rather be frugal and save where I can.

We turn onto the bedding aisle and I let out a cheerful sigh.

"I'm so happy for you, Braelynn," Scarlet says. I told her about the fitted sheet. We're actually here on that mission, although the two hours we spent wandering while chatting and my already half-full cart would say otherwise, and it feels damn good. The aisle is exactly how I pictured it would be. Sheets in all colors and materials.

I let my fingers trail down the row of them as I search for the perfect sheets.

"I think I'm going to get a whole set." The fitted sheet was a small dream. I imagined just one piece of cloth. Enough to make my bed comfortable and not much more. With the check deposited, and a cushion already in savings, I have plenty to get a full set.

We start to wander slowly down the aisle, and I see one and then another that I like. One's an abstract peony in soft muted colors, the other an off-white with a texture to it. "I want to look at them all before I decide," I tell Scarlet, although it's more me to myself so I don't grab every single one that strikes my fancy.

"Do you work today?" she asks.

"Yes," I murmur, running a sample of a flannel set between my fingers. It's very soft, and it would probably be too hot for my place. Flannel sheets aren't necessarily year-round sheets. More of a winter item. A bit expensive, I think to myself ... but then I remember. I can have any set of sheets I want.

"You working every day now?" Scarlet hands me another set to look at. I take my time with it. My shift isn't until this evening, every night at six, so there's absolutely no rush. I nod to her, and she smiles. "He must really like you."

"It's intense," I find myself admitting. It doesn't seem like a good thing or a bad thing to say, just a neutral description of how Declan is. "He's intense."

"I think everybody at The Club would agree with you," Scarlet murmurs. "All the Cross brothers are like that.

They're all broody, my way or no way ... is he like, all gruff all the time?"

A bit of nervousness creeps into my thoughts. "I know he's trying with me." I think of him coming into my apartment with takeout and insisting on talking. It had to be hard for him.

Men like Declan don't have the chance to grow up talking about emotions and apologizing, hell a lot of people don't live with that simple comfort. I know I'm one of the luckier ones only because of my mother. But men like Declan? Hell no. They grow up focusing on survival above everything else. Simply living to see the next day. I know it wasn't easy for him to sit with me and say he was sorry for how things had gone ... and then do it again the next day. "It takes a lot for a man like him, but he's working at it."

"So you two are really involved, then?"

I don't answer her. Mostly because I'm not exactly sure and I don't want to ask. I don't want to be given an answer that pops the bubble of content that I'm in. We look through several more sets of sheets. I'm excited to choose one, but at the same time ... I'm wondering something else. I'm wondering where Declan sleeps. I wonder what his bedroom is like, and whether he likes sheets in a dark hue or a light one. If he likes a comforter that's big and fluffy or heavy. These are the simple things about a person that are impossible to know unless you actually go to his house and sleep in his bed.

I know there's a sofa by the bookshelves that pulls out in

his office, right near the full bath and I know he's stayed in his office more than once. But that's not his home. I have no idea what his home looks like.

"You not going to answer?"

"What?" I peek up and Scarlet's fists are on her hip, pushing in the baggy cream sweater she wears. Even with it not being formfitting, she looks small under the sweater. With black leggings she appears casual and laid back, unlike her raised brow.

"I asked if you guys were really involved," she questions with a knowing smirk.

"Yeah ... we're ... involved more than just sex, I think."

"Like he could take you home one day and show you off at a family dinner?"

My stomach flutters at the thought of that. "Does it scare you?" Scarlet questions when I don't answer.

I remain silent. I don't want to talk about the things that scare me. I run my fingertips over a set of sheets with a high thread count and then I look at the price tag. My eyes go wide. I've never spent that much money on sheets.

"What's going on, Braelynn? If you won't tell me, let me see your phone."

"There's nothing on it." We reach the end of the aisle and turn around. There's a whole other side to choose from. The sheets on this side are pricey at this end and will get cheaper as we go back down. Pink? No, maybe not, though it is a gorgeous pale color. It's quite girly and I'm not sure I want my first place to look … childish. And it could absolutely come off childish if I go with pink. So the sheets go back and I keep looking. I don't want anything satin. I would feel like I was about to slide off the bed.

"No dick pics?"

I choke on a sip of my latte and have to pat my chest to get the coughing to stop. I can't imagine what kind of pictures Declan would send to me … or take of me. The things we do together don't lend themselves to cute selfies that you share with your friends. Scarlet laughs at me. "Okay, no pics. Let me see the messages, then. How is he texting you?"

I unlock my phone, find his name in the list of messages, and hand it over to her. My heart races. This is something I'm used to doing with girlfriends. We all hand around our phones and analyze the texts that men send to us. But this feels different. It's Declan, and Scarlet works for him too. "It's simple," I tell her, as if in apology. I'm not really apologizing. He's not a man who goes on and on in texts.

"Love is in the details," she says, shaking her hair back away from her face. "You keep looking at the sheets and let me look at these."

I try to go back to shopping, but I can't stop stealing glances at her and gauging her expression. I want to know if she sees something that I missed in the messages Declan has sent me.

The way I feel for him obscures a lot. It's confirmation bias, we see what we want to see. I'm sure I do. There's a constant lurking fear of his world and all the darkness that lies there, but as soon as I see his name on the screen, heat overwhelms me. I want him to text me so much that I could have missed red flags. Scarlet scrolls and scrolls, not giving away anything although at one point she narrows her eyes. I lift another set of sheets off the shelves and close my eyes. I try to imagine slipping into bed between them, but instead something else pops into my head. Declan, his arms crossed over his chest and a half grin on his face, looking down at these sheets. On my bed. Maybe he would turn back the covers and run his hand over them too. *What did you buy these for, little pet?* he would ask.

A shiver runs down my shoulders and I fucking love it.

I open my eyes again and look at Scarlet. She has the straw of her Starbucks in her mouth. The cup is in one hand and my phone is in the other. I'm about to say something when the phone rings.

"Shit." Scarlet's face goes white, all the color draining away in an instant. "Oh my God." She's really shaken. The ringer isn't loud, but there is a good volume to it. I had it off silent so I could use it for an alarm this morning. She almost drops her drink, but catches it at the last second and shoves the phone back into my hand.

"It's okay, it's okay," I say, trying to laugh it off and

lighten the mood. "It's an unknown number. We won't worry about it."

"That scared the shit out of me," Scarlet says, and I know it did. She runs a hand through her hair. She paces away from her cart and leans against the shelves. "Just about gave me a heart attack." It takes her a minute to shake it off.

"Are you okay?" I question her although she's starting to seem a little crazy. It was just a phone ringing ... not a gunshot or something intense happening at The Club.

"I'm completely fine," Scarlet says, attempting to play it off. "And he doesn't give shit away. I could like, literally hear his voice in those texts." Before I can respond she adds, pushing her own cart behind mine, "You should also learn the art of sexting."

"How about we look at the rest of the sheets, instead?" I joke and just like that, it's all back to free and easy and putting thoughts of Declan on hold.

We spend another fifteen minutes in the bedding aisle. I go with a set of cream sheets with a higher thread count than anything I've bought before. They have a soft cotton feel, no slippery satin, and they're somehow lightweight and sturdy at the same time. It's going to feel freaking amazing to sleep on these. I also pick out a new comforter, a high-end one that I could absolutely see in an expensive hotel, in a coordinating color, just a slightly darker cream from the sheets but with that texture that caught my eye earlier, and new pillowcases.

"Your bedroom is going to be the lap of luxury," Scarlet says. She has her eye on the sheets too. "I didn't think I wanted new bedding, but maybe I do."

It takes a few more minutes for her to choose a set of her own, and we make our way to the checkout counters. It's a busy day and there's a line. We get into one together, me first, then Scarlet. When I look back at her, she's obviously distracted, biting her lip and staring at the magazines near the back of the line.

"Are you okay?"

Her expressions brightens up and her red lips curve up in a smile. "You're a good friend, Brae. But I'm fine." She waves me off.

I greet the cashier and as she's ringing up my items, my phone buzzes. "I have to warn you," I turn to face Scarlet with the phone raised, "I'm getting a call."

Scarlet laughs. "Go ahead, answer. I'm fine."

I'm expecting it to be another unknown number, or a spam call, but instead it's my mom's name on the screen. "Hi, Mama," I answer quickly. "I'm at the checkout counter at the mall; can I call you right back?"

"Braelynn," she says in a tone that chills my blood.

"Mama, is everything okay?"

Scarlet's gaze whips to mine and I can't pull my eyes away as my mother says, "No, nena," sympathy coating her words.

My stomach goes cold at her tone, and it drops to

the floor. I turn away from the cashier and from Scarlet, wrapping an arm around my stomach and drop my voice. "What happened?"

"I have to tell you some news," she says, her voice shaking. "Is there a place you can sit down?"

# Chapter 19

## Declan

"I won't stay long," I tell Nate as I shrug my jacket over my shoulders. As I'm checking my watch, I add, "Just keep the door open for her, she has plenty of files to sort while she waits."

"I'm sure your brothers will be happy to see you and if anything comes up, let me know."

Slipping my wallet into my back jean pockets, I tell him I will. Home is a good forty minutes away, which is one of the reasons I stay here at night. Too much quiet, too much downtime driving in a car for that long. If I leave now, I'll be there right on time.

I can't help the way my lips pull up at the thought of family dinner. My brother is right, it has been too long.

"I may call her on the way," I say absently, as if I'd need

Nate to tell her that. My good little pet always answers when I message her.

"I'll handle everything here and the pickup from Joshua," Nate says and nods, his hands folded in front of him. It's the first time I've really noticed him all night. He's got a fresh cut and shave, new shoes it looks like too.

"Sharp suit," I compliment him, gesturing toward it with my phone.

Just as he cracks a smile, loosening up to say something, there's a knock on the door, chaotic and demanding, followed by a troubled tone, "Declan."

Before I can answer, my blood chilling, Braelynn barrels into the room. The door wasn't locked. The sight of her is something I didn't expect. It's not time for her to be in and she's dressed in worn jeans and a burgundy sweater that's far too large on her.

Most disturbing, she seems out of breath, her skin drained of color.

"Did you kill Travis?" she whispers with wide eyes before I can say a damn word.

In my periphery, Nate is the one who moves as both Braelynn and I stand perfectly still. The air is tense and each passing second threatens to suffocate me.

"Boss—" Nate attempts to break the tension and I don't spare him a glance as I dismiss him.

He hesitates a half second too long and I speak deathly

low, "Get out." My gaze is still pinned on my little pet who stares back at me, caught and unable to move.

Nate is silent as he leaves, his pace quick enough for me this time. He gives Braelynn a wide berth and as the door closes, she asks again, "Did you ... did you?"

"Did I what?"

The door closes with a harsh click signaling we're alone, and it's Braelynn's undoing. Tears brim in her eyes as she shakes her head in denial. She knew who I was and what I was capable of.

"Do not ask questions I'm unable to answer. I dislike that behavior greatly." Taking a single step forward, she takes one back. There's not much room for her in the least and with one more step, her back hits the door.

I gentle my tone, attempting to comfort her as I near closer, each step careful. "I don't like men who hit women."

"It was years ago," she protests.

"You think you were the last? Men don't change. All they do is wait to show themselves again."

With a harsh swallow, her tears fall, slipping down her cheeks. Her body sags slightly and she looks anywhere but at me.

"This isn't what I wanted," I confess to her, an anxiousness I'm not used to overwhelming me. "What do you need from me?"

She answers me quickly enough, "I don't know."

"I need you to think of something because I don't think you're going to enjoy my response if you don't give me something to do right now." The floor creaks as I stop in front of her, my faces inches from hers as I grip her chin and bring her dark brown eyes back to mine.

They beg me, but I don't know what for.

"I don't know," she says just beneath her breath.

"Come here," I command, opening up my arms. I don't know what she mourns for. The loss of a former lover, or the knowledge that her current is a murderer, either way, she seeks comfort in my grasp.

My arms fold around her as she buries her head into my chest. Kissing her hair, I murmur to her that she's a good girl for obeying.

Her body trembles and I rock her slightly as she calms herself.

"Are you scared?" I ask her the moment her breaths are even.

"I don't know."

"You're going to need to know something, my little pet." Pulling away just slightly, I force her to look up at me. "You're smarter than this," I tell her.

"More shocked than scared." Her gaze drops before coming back up to confide in me, "But yes, you scare me." I can barely breathe at her admission.

"Will you miss him?" My hand cups her cheek and with her answer, her small hand lays against mine.

"No."

"Did you think I should have let him live after hurting you?" With my question her hand drops, and I hate it.

"You can't go around killing—"

"Yes I can. And I will." My tone is brutal and it seems to strike her. Again, I hate it. Anger brims. She didn't even need to find out the man was dead. He was meant to disappear and be gone forever. My declaration is final. "Any man who hurts you, won't live to do it again."

She doesn't cry, she doesn't object. She doesn't even appear to hold on to fear as my words register.

"If we're going to do this, my little pet, you're going to have to get very comfortable with a number of very uncomfortable things. I'm not changing and you knew who I was. I know you did. So let that sink in. If you're mine, then what I am is yours. There's no compromise there. I thought we already covered this. Braelynn, do you know who I am?" I ask her and she merely nods, her eyes still searching mine.

"And do you know who you are to me?"

"Your pet," she whispers.

"You are mine to take care of, and I will do that in the way I know how. Do you understand?"

With her eyes still reddened, but the tears long gone, she answers, "Yes."

"Now come here, or walk away. This is the last time I offer you that. Is that also understood?" I can't explain why the invitation to leave me slipped out. I wish I could take it back. Nervousness pricks at the back of my neck as she answers, "Yes."

I take a half step back, unwilling to turn around. I'm all too aware that I'm scared if I were to turn my back, she could run.

"I will not hurt you or chase you if you decide to—"

"I'm not leaving you." She swallows thickly, her hands closing into fists before opening again. She looks back up at me, "I knew who you were." Her voice tightens and she clears it.

"You were stunned."

"I didn't know," she says and closes her eyes, her shoulders sagging slightly and she doesn't finish the thought.

"I don't want you to mention things like you just did, unless you must."

She nods without peering up at me.

My phone goes off, a text from my brother.

*Fuck.*

Glancing between my phone and a very lost Braelynn, I text my brother I won't be making it tonight.

There's no fucking way I could sit still ruminating over what just happened.

Her softly spoken question catches me off guard as my brother's incoming text comes in. "Was it quick?"

"Does it matter?"

She blinks once before shaking her head. "I guess not,"

she whispers, her voice tight. Again she seems out of place standing there, absorbing not only what I've done, but also what she won't be leaving.

I'll be damned if she can walk away after this. I gave her a chance. One more than I should have.

After tossing my phone that pings and vibrates with another unread message, onto the corner chair, I loosen my tie.

"Strip down and lie on the desk."

Peering up at me, she gives a short nod before obeying. Her movements are slow, but steady.

My tie falls to the floor as she passes me, and every small sound is exaggerated. My blood rushes in my ear as my hand slips to the small of her back. She leans into the touch, glancing over her shoulder. Her dark eyes meet mine and I can't wait for her to strip down and lay out how I like her. My arm wraps around her waist and I pull her into me, crashing my lips against hers.

Her hands grip my shoulders, pulling me in close. *Thank fuck.*

"Declan." She whispers my name but in only moments she'll be moaning, screaming it even. I tear at her clothes and she clings to me.

When I finally plunge deep inside of her, I groan, "Mine," and her legs wrap around my hips, keeping me there as she kisses me. *She* kisses *me*. Finding my lips, devouring them, and loving me how she should.

# Chapter 20

## Braelynn

Secretary work hasn't ever been my ... desired profession. All Declan really has me doing is copying and pasting numbers, filing away invoices. It's nothing dramatic and nothing that requires much thinking. Occasionally some numbers don't add up and I send it to some admin email to review. I'm not certain who it goes to, but whoever it is replies that they'll take care of it each and every time.

It's none of my damn business as far as I'm concerned. In the corner of Declan's office, propped up on the leather high-back chair, I click away, making progress every day and waiting for ... more pleasurable orders. Half of me wonders if Declan even needs me to do this. Or if he simply wants me occupied while I wait for him.

Usually I can get myself to concentrate on the numbers and the records, but tonight it's impossible. I can't focus. My heart pounds thinking of what he did. A hollow pit has opened up inside me and it seems to be taking over my whole body. Every breath I take makes that pit feel more frozen, heavier and as if it'll stay like that forever.

I contributed to a death.

There's no way of avoiding it or denying it. If I hadn't told Declan about Travis, then Travis would still be alive. A chill flows down my shoulders. There's no question of it in my mind. Once Declan knew, he wouldn't allow Travis to keep living. Knowing that I caused this to happen leaves a place inside of me empty.

The thing that makes the emptiness stark and almost shocking is that I should be ... sadder, or scared. More terrified and regretful. I should be shaken to the core that Travis is dead, and that I caused it to happen.

But I'm not. I'm glad he's gone.

With a deep, steadying inhale, I acknowledge the truth. I'm glad he's dead. I have some remorse, but not enough to make me feel as though I'm a terrible person.

My mom didn't raise me to take revenge on people. She wanted me to be able to stand up for myself. She wanted me to be able to set boundaries with others and keep myself safe. But revenge was never the way we lived our lives. "It takes too much of your precious energy, nena," she'd tell me. "Make your life better. Don't make other people's lives worse."

She wasn't talking about killing a person. That's not making their life worse, it's ending it completely.

I push the laptop away, leaving it on the ottoman and pace. My gaze constantly focuses on the closed office door, as if I could will Declan to come back.

I need a break. I need something to distract me. I need him. He can make this feeling go away. He did it last night and he can do it again now. I just need him.

With my fingers making knots around each other, I look through the shelves on the walls, through classic books, eyeing collectibles that look like they've come from all over the world. It seems ... curated. Expensive and luxurious. There's a hint of Declan within the details, but it's not quite him. Vaguely I wonder if he's even read these books, or if he simply prefers to collect them.

The things that are more obviously Declan are tucked away where no one else can see. In the hidden room concealed by the bookshelf. I do two more slow laps around the office, checking for anything else to occupy my time, all the while waiting for him. Anything at all.

I shouldn't be snooping, I know that, but the hidden door begs me to open it. It promises me he won't mind if I wanted to look through the collection of leather implements.

My resistance gives way as the clock *tick*, *tick*, *ticks*, and I open it just like Declan did, pressing my hand against a panel, and all the whips and paddles he showed me before are revealed.

*Holy shit.* Heat engulfs my body. It's no less intimidating now that I'm alone.

I don't dare touch a single thing, but I have time to trace my eyes over the whips and toys and tools. He has an impressive collection and my pulse flutters in my throat. He won't hesitate to use these on me. Probably all of them.

I swallow hard. Some of the whips look vicious. The other implements make me just as nervous, though Declan promised me he knows how to use them. We've done enough together that I believe him. Even staring at the sharp ends of the whip, a heat pools between my thighs. He could make any pain turn to pleasure.

I'd let him do whatever he wanted to me. In this moment, I'm certain of that.

Gaining courage, I take a thick vibrator out of the shelf and test the weight in my hands. Glancing behind me, I have to move around the shelf to check the door. Still nothing. I'm still alone. Placing the vibrator back, I decide to let my curiosity guide me.

I let my mind wander through the various scenarios that would be inspired by each one when I hear someone in the hall, the footsteps steady and sure. The nipple clamps fall to the floor. *Fuck!*

I snatch them up, making sure I haven't left anything

out when I hear the door open. Shit, shit, shit. There's someone with him.

The space is large enough to stand in and like a child caught snooping, I barely get the door closed in time. My heart races in the dark space. There's only a crack of light and it takes my eyes a moment to adjust. The door is not all the way shut. Just enough that I don't think they can see me.

I can't see the door, but I hear it shut and the scooting of a chair. Oh my God. Why did I hide in here? Inwardly I curse myself.

I take a step back into the closet but my shoulder blades brush against the whips hanging on the wall. No more moving, or else I'm bound to push an item off a hook and give myself away. Through the thinnest crack in the door I can see Nate, standing near Declan's desk, although his back is to me. I hope he doesn't look back here and notice the open door. If he does, he'll probably sense I'm standing right behind it.

"How did the meeting with your brothers go?" Nate asks.

My heart pounds. I sure as hell should not be listening to this. Fuck. I do everything I can to block it out. Fisting my hands by my side and closing my eyes although they don't stay closed for long.

"Not much to update on," Declan answers.

I don't know what to do. I'm not sure if I should come out and reveal myself or stay put. It feels like it's too late to do anything.

As they talk, all I can think is: *fuck, fuck, fuck, fuck, fuck.*

Declan comes across the room and stands in front of his desk. His eyes travel over my empty chair in the corner of the office, and then he glances toward the adjoining bathroom. The door is open. I know it. I left it open.

"Three men were killed during the meet late last night," Nate is saying. "Former Talvery men facing off. I've had some contacts say—"

I move slightly, trying to get a better look at Declan's face. He's shifted his position and is hard to see, but then I get the perfect angle and I do. My heart is racing. I shouldn't be in here. Declan lifts his eyes from the surface of his desk and turns his head.

He's looking right at me. My skin blazes and I can barely breathe.

I stay as still as I've ever stayed, despite my pulse hammering inside my chest. True terror overwhelms me, the kind I should have felt and somehow didn't when I learned he'd killed Travis. He turns back to Nate and doesn't interrupt him. *Did he see me?*

"Blow up the bar on Fifth," Declan says. I think it's where the Talvery men have their meets. I'm not supposed to know about it, though. I'm never supposed to hear anything that is spoken in Declan's office. I know plenty now, though. "Have Patrick and Barrett set up a block away."

"Patrick's not in town," adds Nate.

"What about Dorian? He has experience with sniping, doesn't he?"

Nate nods as my body goes cold. *Sniping? As in shooting them?*

"Fine. Have the two of them set up. Kill any of the higher-ups. No one else. Only the higher-ups." Declan taps his fingers on the desk; I can't see but I can hear it. I've learned he does that when he's thinking. "Spread the word that Aria and Carter's marriage was an alliance and we will keep our promise to everyone who has not betrayed us. Make sure we're giving the impression it was only a few men who we believe should pay for what happened, only the few who gave the orders and that it's been dealt with. Give the men the option to come to us ... and turn on each other."

Nate responds, "Yes, Boss."

"I have work to do. We're finished for now."

Nate leaves quickly. The office door opens and closes with a thud. My thumb runs over my fingers, wanting me to push the door open. But I don't know what I'd say.

I'm not given the option to wait any longer, though.

"You can come out now." His voice is calm and even, yet it sends a fear through me.

"Declan, I—" I speak through the crack, not yet opening it and facing him.

I'm cut off by his order. "Come out now so I can see you."

Swallowing the spiked ball in my throat, I obey him

instantly but my hands tremble. "I didn't mean to—"

"It doesn't matter what you meant. It matters that you were here." Still, his tone portrays a matter-of-factness, no anger, no disappointment.

"I'm sorry."

"Put those away." His gaze travels down to my hands, I hadn't realized I was still holding the nipple clamps. My cheeks heat as I open the door, and I feel Declan's eyes burning into the back of my neck with every move I make. When I'm done I come back to him, standing beside his desk where I know he prefers me.

He stands with his arms crossed over his broad chest, his thumb traveling down his jaw as he assesses me. I've never felt so much like a child in his presence. Struggling to say anything at all, I peer up, waiting for him.

"What did you hear?"

"Nothing." I swallow thickly.

"You mean everything?" His brow cocks.

I nod. "I heard everything."

I expect him to be angry at me, but Declan sits on the edge of his desk, his expression calm. "You know better. What should your punishment be?"

"I don't know." My palms are clammy and my heart races.

With a gentleness I don't expect, he brushes my hair away from my face. "You need to give me better answers, my sweet girl." His hand cups my jaw and he repeats, emphasizing the question, "What should your punishment be?"

My mouth is dry. I can't come up with an answer. I just want him to tell me. "Whatever you think it should be."

"I never did get to fuck you after spanking you," he comments, almost to himself. "The next time you're in here when you don't think you should be, do not hide. Do you understand?"

"Yes."

"You come out immediately."

"Yes, Sir."

"Good girl." His voice is a soothing balm. As his thumb runs down my chin and lower, my eyes close. "I prefer for you to be my good girl so I don't have to punish you."

With my heart racing, I swallow and then whisper, "I know." When I open my eyes, his hazel gaze is on me, swirling with a dark lust. He's going to spank me; I know he is. With deep breaths, I prepare myself. Remembering the last time, with the ruler, I contemplate begging him to use his hand instead. I swallow down the plea, I will be his good girl. I'll do whatever he wants. Even if the nervous prickling runs over every inch of my skin. The pain will be bad at first but it won't last for more than a day.

"Strip," Declan commands with a deep rumble of desire.

While I take my clothes off, he sets up two stacks of books on his desk. My focus remains entirely on him because I have no idea what the hell he's doing. There are four to five books in each stack and he attempts to make them even.

Nervousness coils in my stomach. I can't stop watching him. As my bra hits the floor, and the chill of the air sends goosebumps down my arms, he meets my questioning gaze. "I've had a very long night already, my little pet, and an even longer day." He pats the desk and tells me, "I have a meeting in a moment and I'm going to need you to lie there."

I move to obey him without hesitation, grateful to not be bent over and bracing myself for a paddle or that damned wooden ruler and Declan stops me, gripping my chin.

"Let me put you how I want you," he says and as he does, he drops his eyes to my lips and then kisses me sweetly before nipping my bottom lip.

He makes me lie down so my feet are propped on the edge of the desk. My spread thighs will be very close to his chair. When I lay back, he puts the stacks of books on either side of my waist and then he puts his laptop over my belly. It's not touching me. He has the edges balanced on the books. Declan sits, adjusting the screen so it faces him.

My nipples are tight with the chill in the air as I lie here, completely bared to him and staring at the ceiling.

I haven't the faintest idea of what he plans for me, but the moment his thumb brushes down on my clit, I gasp and my back arches from the unexpected touch.

I'm rewarded with a rough chuckle before Declan moves my thighs farther apart, adjusting them the way he adjusted his screen. "If you move, they'll see your legs, so don't you dare move."

I stare up at the ceiling, completely unsure, my heart beating out of my chest. "I'll be still," I promise him. Is this all he plans for me?

"I want to play with you during this meeting. You'll be quiet. You won't move." Biting down on my bottom lip, I keep myself from questioning him.

His thumb comes down on my clit again and I suck in a gasp as a spike of pleasure rides through my body.

"You will not make a sound once the meeting starts," warns Declan. "You will not make a move. Understood?"

"Yes, Declan." My body is tense and my bottom lip drops open with another wave of pleasure as he plays with me.

"Not quite a punishment, is it?" he questions.

My head falls to the side as he rubs ruthless circles over my clit. I can barely think; every effort I have goes into remaining still and quiet. "I don't know."

He hums a short, quiet laugh. "Yes, you do. I'm going to toy with you and get you off. Do not interpret this as a reward. I'm giving you the benefit of the doubt, Braelynn, and selfishly enjoying you as I wanted rather than denying myself."

I nod although I then realize he can't see me and say, "Yes, Declan." Declan stands up to look down at me, towering over me, dominating me and appraising me. His eyes burn into mine. "Be my good girl and be quiet. It's about to start."

I repeat myself. "Yes, Declan."

"That's my good girl," he praises me before sitting back down.

The clicks of his keyboard alert me that his hand is busy elsewhere, leaving me wanting as I lie here helplessly.

Voices come on. I don't recognize any of them. One man says something about alcohol sales, and another man corrects him. They go back and forth for a minute, then move on to the next topic. Declan remains silent throughout it, although his chair groans as he readjusts. It seems like a business conversation but I can't pay attention.

Because Declan's fingers are between my thighs. He strokes them through my slit, already slick from his prior play, pausing every now and then to toy with my clit. He tests my entrance with two thick fingers, seeing if I'm wet and then spreading my arousal up to my swollen nub that begs for his attention. My body goes hot and I struggle to stay silent.

As my release heralds its arrival, my thighs tremble. My hands fist at my side and my head thrashes. I don't know if I can stay still. Fuck, please. Stay still.

When he brushes his fingers along my center, my foot slips. *Shit*—I catch it just in time. My thigh doesn't go. My heart races and my eyes widen when his hand stops.

I wait, holding my breath, and after a moment he continues. This time, his efforts are more ruthless, his fingers curling as he enters me, stroking my front wall and bringing me closer to the edge.

I'm so close. So much pleasure has built up between my legs that the next time Declan brushes his thumb over my clit, I come undone. With both of my hands covering my heated face, I pant into my palms, doing everything I can to keep quiet. Declan doesn't stop. He keeps going and more pleasure crashes over me. He groans deep as I come on his fingers again. This time, I moan a little. I can't help it.

Biting down on my bottom lip, I curse myself when he stops again.

This time Declan taps on the keyboard. "Do I need to remind you to be quiet?"

I shake my head.

"Answer me verbally. My mic is muted."

"No. No. I'll be quiet." A cold sweat coats my body as I gather my strength to stay still and quiet.

"Good girl."

When he says that, *I'm his good girl ...* I'm becoming addicted to it.

His fingers trail over me again as he leans back in his chair, gently now, and he brings me so close to the edge that I almost come again within seconds. Then he backs off. He waits until my thighs have stopped trembling and starts again. He edges me ... and again. The minutes stretch out. Ten minutes, or fifteen. A long damn time to be toyed with and to have release after release denied. He constantly touches me and plays with me and I can hardly breathe with how good it feels. The cool desk beneath my shoulders is my only relief. I'm losing myself to the sensation.

My eyes pop open when I hear his zipper being undone, and I wait for him to fuck me, but he just plays with me. Both thighs are trembling now. I can't take much more.

A small moan of protest leaves me, begging him, and then he stops altogether, his touch retreating.

"Excuse me, gentlemen. Just a moment." Declan moves the computer.

Fuck, fuck.

I'm silent as Declan picks me up as if I'm nothing, grasping onto him and wanting to plead with him but I stay silent. He bends me at the waist, his arms bracing me before he lowers me over the arm of a chair. "This is going to be quick," he murmurs in my ear, his warm breath trailing down my shoulder, and then he thrusts into me with all his thick length. It all happens so quickly, I'm barely aware of it until he's inside of me. Declan fucks me hard and deep, using me like the fuck toy he said I would be.

My entire body is weak by the time he comes inside of me and I've come yet again, at least the fourth time since he started all of this.

"Fuck, Braelynn," he murmurs. Declan rests me on the chair, zips his pants up, and goes back to the meeting. The leather is cool beneath me and thank God it's leather because the warmth leaks out of me and onto the chair.

Sated and weak, I clean it up and clean myself off, still attempting to calm my breathing.

When I've finished, Declan pats his lap. I hear, but when I raise my eyes to look at him, he's not looking back. He's casual, though stern, facing the monitor. He pats his lap again and taps on the keyboard, I assume to mute his mic again.

"Come here," he orders. "Crawl if you have to."

Another click on the keyboard.

I obey. I crawl to him, and he pats his knee. I rest my head against it while he pets my hair. His touch is soothing, possessive, yet everything I need. My heavy eyes close as Declan strokes my cheek and time passes allowing me to recover.

There's a clink that forces my eyes open.

A pen dropped, and Declan bends down. I offer it to him, and Declan takes it, his fingers brushing against mine, but he looks deep into my eyes. "Do you need me to hold you?"

I shake my head, taken aback.

"If you did, you'd tell me, wouldn't you?"

"Yes." A simper plays on my lips. "Good." A warmth I haven't felt with him takes over as he kisses me once.

"If you need me, squeeze." He puts my hand on his thigh. "Understood?"

"Yes."

He sits back up and returns to the call, but his hand never stops moving over my hair and that warmth never leaves me.

# Chapter 21

## Declan

She's already seen and heard too much. Most is intentional and a setup, in case she is an informant. The information will identify her and it's not true. But some things ... like the meeting yesterday ... I should not have let her hear that conversation.

My family has only dealt with that particular situation one of two ways.

A quick death or marriage. All their wives have been involved in matters they shouldn't have. And none of them can be forced to testify. If Braelynn isn't an informant, but she hears things she shouldn't ... there's only one of two ways we deal with that.

All morning the consequences of what our relationship

has evolved into have bothered me. They've whispered into the back of my mind that it's going to come to an end. It would protect my little pet. She wouldn't have to worry if she overheard conversations. It's her worrying that's the problem, I've come to decide. I take it as my responsibility to ease that.

Time is not in our favor, but it will certainly help.

*Knock, knock.* My gaze lifts to the door and then to the monitors on my left. I hadn't noticed Nate coming down the stairs.

I call out, "Come in."

Nate closes the door quietly after entering, his custom-tailored suit looking more rumpled than I'm used to seeing on him.

"What is it?" I ask him and then click over to my schedule. The night is nearly free and what I do have on my calendar can be pushed back. Nothing is pressing, so I'm not sure why the hell Nate has that look on his face. There's always a tell about him when he's stressed.

"Your brother called a bit ago."

"What for?"

"He said he wanted a quick conference. He has orders." There's something about Nate at the moment that I don't care for. There's an anxiousness about him.

"Call him," I order him and lean back.

Nate does as directed, calling on his burner. As it rings, my thumb trails over my stubble. If Carter has orders, something's changed.

"Boss," Nate says in greeting as the line is picked up.

"Is my brother there?" Carter questions.

"I'm here," I call out. Nate places the phone down gently on my desk and resumes standing, his hands clasped in front of him.

"Declan." Jase's voice comes through next. I get the impression it's a fucking intervention.

"Fuck, if this is about dinner, it's a bit of overkill." I let out a short laugh, but my brothers are silent. "I'll be there next week."

I bite my tongue before telling him I may bring Braelynn. I'm not certain I should. Things have been difficult and I don't know whether it would make things better or worse to involve my family. I want them to meet her, though.

Carter speaks first. "It worked."

"What worked?" I question and I'm the only one. I take it I'm the last to know.

"Whoever you set up with the numbers."

My blood goes cold and I peek up, Nate doesn't even look at me.

"What numbers?" I ask. They can't be talking about the books. Denial sinks its claws into me, holding me steady as Carter confirms the unwanted thoughts.

"We got in the transcript this morning. We notified Nate in case she came in. Braelynn, isn't it?"

Betrayal sinks deep into the marrow of my bones. My world turns blurry, reality bends and spins in front of me. Taunting me. Laughing at the very thought that I believed her.

She said she wouldn't hurt me.

Every doubt I ever had screams at me, demanding I acknowledge they were right.

Of course she stayed last night rather than leaving. It's the only reason she ever stayed.

"She's working for the feds. Now we know."

Nate's statement brings my focus back.

I clear my voice and sit up straighter, my shoulders stiffening as I tell my brother, "Send me everything. I want to be sure it's her."

"Declan." Carter's tone is reprimanding. "She's the only one—"

My voice is harsh as chaotic anger burns inside of me. "Send it to me."

To keep my hands from trembling, I form white-knuckled fists.

"Declan, the information about the train tracks is in the testimony," Jase tells me. Matter-of-factly, but also with an air of sympathy. If he were here, I know he'd grip my shoulder, then pat it.

He would tell me it's all right, but it's not.

Nothing about this is right.

"The tracks?"

"From our conversation," Nate speaks, and when I look up his eyes are on me but only for a fraction of a second. The moment my gaze narrows, he looks downward, focusing on his shoes instead.

My vitriol has nowhere to hide.

"And the numbers in the books, the ones that were off and you planted. They're in the report."

"It has to be her."

My body sags into the chair. "Get out," I whisper as something else takes hold of me. Something I don't care to admit. "Get out, Nate." When I glance up to scream at him, I realize he's already gone. He left quietly. Smart man I suppose, given I was prepared to throw anything I could find at him.

"Declan? Are you there?" Carter questions.

"I'm here."

"We're coming, all right? We'll be there soon."

I can't explain why, but hearing Carter tell me that breaks something inside of me.

"Are you sure?" I ask him and then I think maybe he would misunderstand and think I'm referencing him coming down here to The Club, but before I can clarify he tells me.

"It's her, Declan. We need to take care of this."

*To take care of it ...* my blood chills. I'm quick to end the call, before the emotions swarm and make me a weaker man.

## Chapter 22

### Braelynn

Every day is the same now, a tempting lullaby. The red door that used to haunt my every thought now leads to my sanctuary.

When I get in, with my purse tucked under my arm and my heels clicking as I go, I stride straight to the office like I always do. Every step brings a new heat, the sweet dull ache reminding me of yesterday.

Declan Cross is insatiable. It does something to me. If nothing else, he wants me. And I crave that from him. Perhaps that's what it's like to be in this kind of relationship. This pining to please him and be pleased by him is addictive. I don't know what the future holds when it comes to men like Declan, but I do know that he can't get enough of me nor I him.

We'll take it one day at a time. That's what I tell myself. That's what anyone else would do. My footsteps still seem to echo from the iron stairs as I approach Declan's door toward the end of the hall. I'll never forget the first time I had to come down here. I knew the power Declan had over me from the first moment our eyes met.

I'm beginning to think that power dynamic will always be the same. Even if the rest of the world goes to shit, the way I feel when Declan looks into my eyes won't go away.

It's an uncertain feeling that overwhelms me at that thought, because I desperately want it to be true, and that's a dangerous thing. I let my shoulders relax and reach for the door. Time to balance the books, or bend over the desk, or sit in his lap and kiss him. Anything could happen tonight, and part of me is excited for that.

Only the door doesn't open for me. I shake the handle a second time. It's locked.

That's strange. For the three weeks I've been working, it's always unlocked. Last week he told me to enter without even knocking.

Balling my hand, I knock on the door with uncertainty. There's a pitter-patter in my chest and I ignore it.

"Declan?" I call his name. No one answers.

After a moment, I take my phone from my purse and open a new message.

*Braelynn: I'm at the office, are you in there?*

Leaning against the wall by his door, I wait. Peering down to my right and then my left. I check my phone and social media ... taking up time. After a few minutes, no new messages appear and I decide to send another one.

*Braelynn: No one's here to let me in. Should I go home or do you want me to stay? I could wait upstairs at the bar if you'd like?*

Something feels off. Very wrong as I wait in the silence. It's an uncomfortable sensation that I can't quite place.

I really don't like this feeling that comes over me. A noise from around the corner grabs my attention. A footstep, maybe. A scuffle of a shoe against the floor. The hairs on the back of my neck stand up. It could be Declan over there, but why wouldn't he have answered me?

Fear creeps up on me as I take a hesitant step forward.

"Declan?" I barely breathe, not trusting the quiet.

I pull my purse higher on my shoulder and move through the hallway. The noise ricochets through the hall again. It almost sounds like a high heel tapping.

A crease settles in the middle of my forehead. "Hello?" I call out, expecting to hear Mia maybe or another waitress.

When I turn the corner near the back room, I see them and my body goes numb. It's a chilling sight and I don't believe what I see.

*Scarlet.*

And Nate, with his hand over her mouth. She's pressed

against the wall, her red dress barely seen around his navy blue suit. I blink and what happens next is over with in a matter of seconds.

The sight of her is paralyzing. Her eyes are wide with terror, and her hands scrabble at his, which are wrapped around her throat. They get even wider when she sees me and her body struggles against Nate's grip. Her mascara leaks down the corner of her eyes with the tears.

My purse drops to my side, my body trembling.

Panic makes my throat go tight, but a survival instinct freezes me in place. One of her heels clicks against the floor. Fuck. She can't even get her feet on the ground. He's choking her!

*Do something!* A voice screams in my head and by the time I'm able to act, it's too late. It all happens in the span of a single breath. By the time I step forward, a scream tearing up my throat, it's over.

"I'm sorry," Nate whispers.

And then he snaps Scarlet's neck. The crack resonates inside of me, paired with the sight of her body going limp, her eyes no longer blinking and her arms falling at her side.

A scream rips out of me, scratching at my throat.

My heart hammers as Nate turns to look at me, without an ounce of sympathy in his expression. With adrenaline surging through me, I turn to run and collide with a hard chest.

My body flinches, and tries to escape until I look up.

Declan grabs me, cold and cruel. He turns me around and pins me close, a hand over my mouth, the other pinning my arms down. "He killed her!" I try to scream, but I can't. "Declan! Please!" My words are muted, my body hot and my entire being filled with terror even though Declan's here. My mind is a whirlwind that won't stop.

*Help her,* is all I can think. Even though I know she's already dead. Tears leak from the corners of my eyes as my throat goes raw with my cries.

Declan turns my head in his hand so I have to look at him. His grip is brutal and it's shocking when I see his face. His eyes hold a deadly anger and everything stills.

Very, very slowly, he removes his hand from my mouth. It's not comforting. He's still holding me too tight. Tight enough to crush me. It's hard to catch my breath. My mind spins back through what just happened.

Scarlet is dead.

My friend. I saw her die. Nate snapped her neck. Killed in cold blood.

"Declan." His name, a plea from me, is barely audible. I can't breathe enough to put my voice behind it. "I'm scared."

"My little pet," he says, and his voice is brutal. I thought I knew fear before but ice spills through my veins. "You should be fucking terrified."

# About the Author

Thank you so much for reading my romances. I'm just a stay at home Mom and an avid reader turned Author and I couldn't be happier.

I hope you love my books as much as I do!

More by Willow Winters
www.willowwinterswrites.com/books

Printed in the USA
CPSIA information can be obtained
at www.ICGtesting.com
JSHW082247240124
55713JS00003B/10